Mail-Order Tailor

Sarah Lamb

A thank you to my proofreader, Brooke, and all of the lovely women who help ARC read to catch those typos I miss!

Paperback ISBN: 978-1-960418-47-0

Large print ISBN: 978-1-960418-48-7

Contents

May you always have a place that eases your heartache.

Chapter 1

1870s Deepwater, Missouri

Josiah Adams couldn't seem to stop touching the letter in his pocket. This entire situation unsettled him. His whole life, he'd never had a drop of impulsiveness. Not a one. So what on earth had compelled him to apply to a mail-order marriage company? And then, to answer their offer and pack up all he had to move to a town he'd never heard of, for the chance of marriage?

His eyes roamed the nearly empty stagecoach, and the hard lines that had been on his face softened when they fell on his young daughter, fast asleep on the hardly cushioned stagecoach bench.

Madeline.

Sweet, darling, cheerful Madeline. Only six years old, she was his pride and joy. His very reason for waking up each morning. That's why.

A lump formed, as it always did when he thought about the last few years and how difficult they'd been. How he'd always had to put on a cheerful face for Madeline, or Maddie, as he called her. The last six years had been long, and there were many times he'd wondered how he'd care for her and run a business that could both grow to give them comfort one day and put food on the table, but somehow things had always worked out.

Josiah held in a sigh as he watched trees roll past, the sun filtering through their canopies and sending beams shooting this way and that. His fingers reached for the letter again. A mail-order husband. He'd never thought to be such a thing. Not until he'd seen the sign in the general store, and the woman working there had suggested that might be a solution to his problem.

"Get wee Maddie a mother," she'd encouraged, "and yourself someone to help look after you too. Don't you think the time has come for such a thing? She's growing up, Josiah. She'll need a woman to teach her things. Especially those men don't understand."

While all of that was true, the idea still felt uncomfortable. A mother. A wife. He wasn't at all sure such a thing could happen, but he'd mailed off a letter at the store owner's urging, enclosed his application fee, and a few weeks later, found himself presented with several options.

He couldn't deny that something pulled him toward the town of Deepwater. He wasn't sure why. He didn't even know much at all about the woman waiting, other than she had been traveling herself to be a mail-order bride, and was stranded there. It felt like the right thing to do, both for his situation and this young woman's, even if it didn't make the least bit of sense logically.

After the agency assured him that his bride would be waiting in the small town of Deepwater, Josiah had told Maddie.

"I get a mommy?" the girl had gasped, her eyes wide. Then she'd run off to pack.

A lump filled Josiah's throat again, just like it had that day. His daughter deserved a mother's love. He'd done the best he could, but he was no substitute for the way a mother could nurture and care for a child.

Maddie had never known her mother. A beautiful, willowy woman, Celina had been too good for him. Yet, she'd married him, a simple tailor, anyway. They'd been happy for a few months, but that was all.

Celina had quickly become unhappy with having to work around their home, and how they struggled at times as he grew his business. She'd been raised for a life of ease, not one of household drudgery and few dresses, she'd reminded him more than once. Her true colors were shown, his mother would have said, had she still been alive to advise him.

A week after Maddie was born, she left, with only a single letter to show she'd ever been there. All of her belongings, and herself, vanished, as though she'd never existed.

I won't be back, the letter had read. *Raise her on your own. This isn't the life I want for myself.*

There was no apology. No hint of love. Not even a message for their helpless daughter, who would have questions about the mother she'd never known as she grew.

A woman in the town had a new babe herself, and had kindly nursed Maddie, ensuring that the innocent infant had the nourishment she needed. Meanwhile, Josiah, almost numb to everything around him, went through the motions of rebuilding his life. His main goal was to provide for and protect Maddie.

And protect her, he did. She was never out of his sight. She played during the day or wrote her numbers and letters in his shop, and she also became handy with a needle and thread, as he let her practice on scraps of fabric.

It would be difficult to let someone else have some say in her care, he mused, staring through the stage window. But he knew it was time. Maddie needed a mother's affections. He hoped very much that this woman he was about to meet would lavish her with the motherly love that she needed.

If she was a woman he could get along with, that would be even better. He wasn't expecting much. Companionship was not even a need, but he hoped it would develop, with someone there sharing his home.

His fingers felt for the letter again. The agency promised that if he and the woman weren't suitable, he could go elsewhere. Or they'd send someone to him. He would hold them to that, even though he hoped he wouldn't need to. As long as the woman was suitable, with a good heart and patience as he'd asked, that was acceptable to him.

Deepwater didn't actually sound like too bad of a town. He'd written to the church there, and the reverend had replied almost right away, telling him about the town, and even how there was a vacant building the printer used to own that would be perfect for him to use to set up his own tailor shop—and that they were in sore need of one.

That made him feel better. A place that seemed welcoming, and was in need of his skills, would be a good place to settle. To start fresh. Get away from all the memories. He just hoped that everyone was as kind as this Reverend Gabriel Sullivan seemed to be. The one thing he didn't want was to be looked down on.

It was awkward enough being a mail-order husband. Then, having to explain that he was one not because his wife had passed away, but because she'd abandoned him?

He didn't want the pity. Didn't want Maddie to carry that shame on her shoulders. It was bad enough he did.

For years, he'd wondered what he could have done differently. Said differently. No matter some told him that it wasn't his fault, that's just how she was. Others had come along and asked how hadn't he known that would happen? Him, a simple tailor, and she, a beautiful woman with dreams. They weren't suited, and how could he have ever thought he would be able to make a woman like her happy?

Josiah's chest felt tight with the painful memories. It only eased when the stage started to slow and he glanced toward Maddie, who was starting to awaken. He let out a slow breath, trying to remind himself that the past was behind him, and he was facing his future.

It was a shame it never worked. His failures and fears would follow him wherever he went, as though he'd packed them in one of the many trunks on the stage.

"We are almost there," he told Maddie, and then wrapped his arm around her small shoulders as she joined him at the window to glance curiously at the town that would be their new home.

Small buildings on the outskirts grew denser, and they passed a small wooded area, then a large white church. Not a moment later, the driver called, "Deepwater! Here we are!"

When the stage stopped and the passenger door opened, Josiah took a deep breath, his first in this small town of Deepwater, and felt the strangest thing settle over him.

Hope.

Chapter 2

Eager to escape the teasing laughter behind her, Ginny Waters shut the kitchen door and headed toward the general store to get the items on her mother's list. Her hand squeezed the basket's handle, and she used the slightly painful sensation to distract her from the ache the teasing had caused.

She was sure her younger sister hadn't meant to call her a spinster. Unwanted. Undesired. She was simply trying to make herself feel better as she showed off her new dress, talking about how it would attract the attention of someone she liked.

That didn't mean it hurt any less. Nor did the sympathetic looks she got from some of the older women in town, along with the question of when she'd be getting married.

Ginny was quite aware she had very little hope for the kind of future she'd dreamed of. She thought she'd have been married long before now. It wasn't that she didn't enjoy living at home, but at nearly twenty-five, she wanted to find her own way in life. She'd always thought that meant being a wife and eventually a mother, then running her own household.

In Deepwater, however, that had been a little difficult to make happen. While most of her friends had married and seemed happy, there wasn't anyone for her. Yet. That seemed to be her mother's favorite word. Ginny was sure it was meant to comfort her, but instead, the three letters taunted her.

It was always *yet*. No beau, yet. No job, yet. No escape from the constant teasing of her younger sister, yet.

Would her sister, almost nineteen, be married before she was? Ginny had always thought she would be wed before her youngest sisters, but every day, that seemed less likely, especially as both her younger sisters had young men who kept stopping by and taking them on walks.

What would it be like to be wanted in a romantic sense? Ginny wished she knew. She longed to feel desired. Needed.

In truth, Ginny was *needed*. But it was at home. Not by a sweetheart. Her mother struggled greatly to help her father on the farm, since Ginny's older brothers had married already. Now, it was just her, plus her two younger sisters at home.

Her mother understood, and was even apologetic that Ginny had to do so much, but as neither an opportunity for employment nor marriage had come her way, it wasn't like Ginny had anything else to fill her days with. Besides, she loved her family, both her parents and siblings, even if she did long for just a little romantic opportunity beyond what was afforded her.

Letting her eyes roam, Ginny tipped her face skyward. It was too beautiful of a day to worry. A gentle breeze rustled the deep green leaves on the tall oaks and maples, and the faint scent of the pines filled her nose. It was the most perfect of summer days, and she knew she'd enjoy every moment of it.

As she walked past the post office, someone called her name. Ginny stopped, and turned toward the open window. "Hello!" she greeted Peter, the postmaster.

"There's a letter for your father," he told her. "Do you want to take it? It looks like it's from your brother."

"Yes, I'll be sure he gets it," Ginny said, accepting the envelope. "I hope you are well? And Alyssa?"

Alyssa and Peter had married a little over a year earlier. She had been a mail-order bride who'd been rejected on the spot. The man's loss, however, was Peter's gain. They were a wonderful couple, and Ginny liked them both.

"She's great," he told her. "Gone to get us a bite at Maggie's Café."

"Yum!" Ginny patted her stomach and smiled, then waved goodbye, heading toward the store.

As she neared it, she spotted a little girl, of perhaps six, running from one side of the street to the other. Ginny tipped her head to the side as she observed her. She'd never seen the child before. At least, as far as she could recall.

Dark pigtails hung on the girl, and her dress was pink with flowers on it. As Ginny drew closer, she saw worry on the child's face, and it tugged at her.

"Papa? Papa!" The last was said on a sob.

"Are you lost?" Ginny called, and increased her speed.

"I'm not," the little girl said, her eyes as dark as her hair. "Papa is."

Ginny couldn't help but smile. She liked that perspective. As a child, it was likely one she'd have had. "Would you like help to find him?" she asked.

The girl hesitated, then nodded. "Yes. Please."

"I'm Ginny," Ginny told her.

"Madeline Adams. But you can call me Maddie." The girl gave her an adorable smile.

"Are you traveling through on the stage?" Ginny asked. "Perhaps your papa is at the station."

"We were on it," Maddie said, then crinkled her nose. "But we got off of it, because this will be our home now.

I'm going to have a *mother*," she added proudly, putting emphasis on the word.

"That's wonderful," Ginny answered with a smile. She didn't quite understand what the girl meant, but her acknowledgment made the child smile even brighter.

Just then, a man with dark hair and spectacles and clutching a small bag ran toward them. "Maddie!" he called.

"Papa! There you are," the little girl said. She turned back to Ginny. "Thank you for helping me. I have him now," her sweet voice said.

"It was my pleasure," Ginny assured her.

The man had come to them, and wrapped an arm around his daughter. "Hello," he said with a nod to Ginny. "Josiah Adams. Maddie is mine. We've just arrived, and got separated for a moment."

"Welcome to Deepwater," Ginny said.

"Thank you," Josiah said. "Though we've just gotten here, everyone seems very kind, and I'm looking forward to being part of the community."

"Papa is a tailor," Maddie said. "He does wonderful work."

"Is that so?" Ginny asked. "Then I'm sure you will be very busy soon. We've a dressmaker, but no tailor. The men will be most glad to have you."

Josiah seemed almost shy as he glanced around. "I hope that is the case. It is always a little difficult starting over."

"Maddie mentioned her mother," Ginny said. "I look forward to meeting her."

"As do I," Josiah said. Then he stammered, "What I mean is, we don't know her. I came to marry a woman here. And, well..."

When he didn't say anything more, Ginny simply nodded. "Well then, I wish you all the happiness."

"Could you point me to the café?" Josiah asked hurriedly. "I was told to get the key to our new home there."

"Yes, you are right near it," Ginny told him, and motioned to the café, just a few doors away. "Maggie is the owner. I'm sure she will be able to help."

"Thank you," Josiah said. "Come along, Maddie." Then he turned back to her. "Nice to meet you, Miss..."

"Ginny Waters," she told him with a smile. "Just Ginny, please."

"Ginny." He nodded, and then he and his daughter turned away.

For a moment, Ginny watched them, and then continued to the store. She wondered when she'd see them again. Since Deepwater was so small, everyone knew everyone, and a newcomer would quite quickly be the focus of attention. She hoped that they'd feel welcome here. More than that, she wondered just who it was he'd come to marry. As far as she knew, there wasn't anyone in town expecting a mail-order husband.

Perhaps that was what she should consider, Ginny mused. A mail-order marriage. After all, many did find happiness with them. But could she leave Deepwater? Ginny loved being here in this town. Perhaps she could send away for a husband then, like someone else had obviously done?

Whatever woman ended up with Josiah Adams would be fortunate indeed. He seemed like a kind man, and it was obvious he loved his daughter. A man like that, and one who had his own business, would make a fine husband for any woman.

He was also quite attractive, if one thought about it. He'd be better looking if he didn't have those worry lines between his eyebrows, but Ginny decided that was just his concern over losing his daughter for a moment. His eyes were warm and kind. And his voice...it had been very pleasing to her ears.

Ginny pushed open the door to the store, glancing over her shoulder just in time to see Josiah and his daughter walk into the café. For some reason, a tiny pang of envy went through her just then. Just as quickly, she scolded herself. She shouldn't be thinking such things about another's intended.

Yes, whoever married him would be a very lucky woman indeed. She just hoped that one day, she'd get to experience marriage with a man like him, and a daughter as sweet as Maddie seemed to be.

Chapter 3

When Maddie had been missing, even though it was only for a moment, Josiah had been in a panic. After he'd spotted her, standing next to a young woman with a sweet face and a gentle smile, he should have been relieved. But instead, as he hurried over, he was filled with fear. New to the town, what would the woman think of him and his inability to care for his child?

He'd nearly been speechless when Ginny had mentioned Maddie spoke of her mother. It had been slightly embarrassing to admit that he was there for a mail-order marriage. What would she think of him?

Josiah figured he needed to stop thinking like that, especially if Deepwater, which appeared to be a nice little town, was to be his new home.

A small bell jangled over the door of the café as Josiah pushed it open. Maddie skipped in front of him, over to a glass case that had pies, cookies, and loaves of bread in it.

"Hello," a woman greeted them. "I'm Carissa. How can I help you?"

"Hello," Josiah said. "My daughter and I have just moved here. I'm Josiah Adams. I've purchased the old print shop. I was told you have the key?"

"Yes, we do. Dirk, he's the printer, asked us to hold it for you, while he and his wife Samantha are away for a few days. Just a moment." Carissa disappeared through a door that Josiah assumed led to the kitchen, and a moment later returned with an envelope. "Here you are," she said. "It is in here, along with a note from him."

"Thank you," Josiah said.

"Papa," Maddie said, in a whisper that wasn't very quiet. "Can I have a cookie?"

"If it's fine with your father, I'd love to gift you one, as a welcome-to-Deepwater treat," Carissa said, smiling at them.

"Oh, thank you," Josiah said.

"That one?" Maddie asked, pointing to a sugar cookie.

"That very one," Carissa promised, and picked up the cookie in a bit of brown paper, handing it to her.

"Thank you," Maddie said.

"Yes, thank you," Josiah said. "That was very kind of you."

"If you need anything, please let me know," Carissa said. "My aunt Maggie is usually here, and she and my uncle Hank know just about everything. Both about Deepwater, and the people here."

"Oh! That's wonderful. I wonder if you can help me," Josiah began. "I'm looking for a woman who had placed an ad for a mail-order husband. It sounds foolish, I know, that I don't have a name for her, but the letter from the mail-order agency was damaged when I got it. However, the date to arrive here was stated, and I was told I could learn more at this very café, so I came."

"I'm sorry," Carissa said, shaking her head. "I really don't know. My aunt might. She'll be back in a few hours if you want to stop by?"

"Thank you," Josiah said. "I will do that."

He took Maddie by the hand and led her outside. They walked back to the stage station.

"Got your key?" the man asked.

"I do," Josiah said. "Is there someone I can pay to bring our trunks?"

"I'll get them there, no charge," the man assured him. "Be about an hour."

"That's just fine," Josiah said, and opened the envelope for the key. There was a note inside that directed him to the building, and a few moments later, Josiah was putting the key into the lock.

The building was two stories. The front would allow for a nice store, with an ample work area. Up the stairs were two rooms that would serve as bedrooms, and a small kitchen and sitting area. It would do very nicely.

Josiah had been a little concerned about buying the place sight unseen, even if the letters he'd exchanged seemed to give all of the necessary information, but knowing that the bride he was to marry didn't have a home already meant that he'd need to have something. Especially if things didn't work out, and he and the woman decided they were not compatible.

"Which room is mine?" Maddie asked.

"You may choose whichever you'd like best," Josiah told her.

He watched with a smile as his daughter explored, then decided on which she wanted. The rooms were near identical in size, so he didn't mind letting her pick.

There was a knock at the door, and he went downstairs to see their six trunks there. He brought them inside, one for Maddie, one for him, and four with the things he needed for his shop, such as tools, fabric, and sundries. Once he was set up, he could specially order his materials, but he couldn't very well open a store with nothing on hand, so he'd brought enough to get started.

As Josiah started right away to set up his storefront, Maddie came down the stairs. "Papa, can I sit outside?"

"Better not," he told her. "Not without me. Tonight we can have dinner at the café, and we will walk around a little afterward."

"But that's so long away," Maddie complained. "I'm bored."

"Yes, but we are also new to this area, and I don't want you to get lost," Josiah said. "Why don't you unpack your trunk and make sure your doll settles in?"

With a sullen nod, Maddie went upstairs, and Josiah continued unpacking. He felt a little bad. It had been a long journey, and he knew that Maddie was likely bored. But he couldn't let her roam around on her own. No matter that this was to be their new home and Deepwater didn't seem so large she could get lost.

What if something happened to her? He had spent his whole life trying to protect her. If something happened to his daughter, he didn't know how he'd manage. Which was why he was all the more anxious to find the woman he was to marry. Maddie wasn't content to play by his side all the time anymore. She'd been sneaking away more and more as of late. He needed a second pair of eyes to help him with her before she wandered off and got hurt.

Not for the first time did unease wash over him at the idea of a marriage of convenience. He tried to tell himself, as he always did, that there was nothing wrong with one. In fact, many had proven successful, so the odds were good that this one would be too.

Besides, after his experience with Celina, and how he'd been so head over heels in love with her he'd missed all the signs that things weren't right, it was likely better this not be a love match.

A couple walked past the window just then, laughing and holding arms with each other. Josiah turned away, refusing to acknowledge the stabbing pain in his chest at the sight. He was done with love. Had been for years. You couldn't trust it. It made people blind. Foolish in their ways. No more. There was only one thing that mattered to him—protecting his daughter. And that included getting her a mother who wouldn't leave again.

Chapter 4

Ginny browsed the large collection of books in the café. Like everyone else in the town, she'd been very excited when they'd not only been able to replace the school children's books after a fire, but also had enough extra to buy more than a hundred books for the café to create their own town library. Once a month, a new title, sometimes two, were added, and the collection of books was a treasure beloved by all in the community.

The shelves along the sitting area of the café were filled with books of all kinds. There were fairy tales and dime novels, books on history and nature, poetry and literature, and even copies of the town's Christmas book they'd worked together to create. There was something for everyone.

And this was a place Ginny enjoyed visiting each week, and choosing a title to take home with her. Sometimes, she would enjoy a mug of cider and a cookie or slice of pie from the café. Other times, she'd just take a book with her.

Today, Ginny browsed the shelves, letting her fingers glide over the spines. She settled on a novel, and carefully wrote her name and the title on a piece of lined paper that served as the checkout for the library.

"See you later," she called to Maggie, who waved in return, and then Ginny left, planning to stop for a short time at one of the benches along the stream and read a chapter or two.

She walked through the town, catching sight of the new man pacing in front of his shop.

Josiah.

He was a bit of a mystery to her. Though he'd been there a week now, he rarely left his shop, and though he said he'd come to wed, she'd not seen a woman there. Without any need to visit a tailor, she hadn't had a chance to just poke her head in. He also seemed to keep to himself. This past Sunday, right after the church service, he and his daughter had left before anyone had a chance to speak to him.

While the people of Deepwater weren't exactly gossiping about him, they were all quite curious. Ginny was no exception. But that was simply because a new person was interesting, and in a small town, novelty was always exciting.

"Ginny! Wait a moment!"

She turned, and then smiled at Laura, the reverend's wife, who was about her age, and waited as she crossed the street. "It's a fine afternoon, isn't it?" Ginny said by way of greeting.

"It is indeed." Laura sighed happily and looked upward. "Not a cloud in the sky. I love the sunshine. How have you been?"

"Good," Ginny said. "I stopped to get a book after I visited the store to look for employment."

"Still looking?" Laura asked sympathetically. "It's times like these I wish the town weren't so small. There aren't always enough jobs for those who seek them. Women, anyway."

"I don't really need the work," Ginny admitted. "You know my parents keep all of us busy. It's just more that I may never marry. I've realized that. The time will come I'll need to be independent. To do that, some money saved and a steady income will be needed."

"I understand," Laura assured her. "But you must not get yourself worried over your future, if you'll marry or not. I sense the right man will come along for you."

"Excuse me, Mrs. Sullivan?" Josiah came up to them, and stammered, "I don't mean to interrupt, but might I have a word?"

"Of course," Laura answered. "But remember, it's Laura. Not Mrs. Sullivan."

"Forgive me," the tailor said. Then he nodded at Ginny. "It's good to see you again."

"And you," Ginny answered. "I'll leave you two to talk."

"Oh, it's not private," Josiah quickly said. "In fact, perhaps you can both help." He glanced behind him at his shop, then back at the women. "You see, I've not been able to find the woman I was to marry. In fact, it seems there isn't a woman in the town who was waiting for a husband. I still don't know who requested me. Maggie didn't either."

"How strange," Laura murmured.

"I don't want to be married so much for myself," Josiah said quickly. "But for my daughter. I had hoped for a caregiver for her. She needs a woman's influence and care as she's getting older. My shop is quite busy, and as there is no school right now, I need someone to help watch her. Perhaps even cook. While I wait a time longer for whoever sent the letter, I still need help with my daughter. Would either of you know of a woman willing to assist me?"

Ginny's eyes widened, and she glanced at Laura, who raised her eyebrows. Ginny gave the smallest of nods, a spark of hope filling her. A job! And one with sweet Madeline and her father? That wouldn't be any trouble at all. And, if she was quite truthful, it wasn't just the job that had her feeling a hint of excitement, but it was a chance to be around Josiah a little more. She couldn't explain it, but ever since she'd met him, it had been hard to not think about him.

"I could help you," Ginny blurted out. "I have a lot of experience both with children and with cooking."

"It's quite true," Laura said with a nod. "Ginny is one of eleven."

"Are you sure?" Josiah asked, furrowing his brow. "It's not that I don't think you are capable. I just thought, perhaps, an older woman..."

She tried not to feel disappointed. Despite what he'd just said about not thinking her incapable, that's just how his words made her feel.

Ginny had opened her mouth to reassure him she'd be more than suitable, when he added, "And it's just temporary, you see. At least, I think so. I don't want to disappoint you if the woman does show up soon, and takes over those duties. Being so new to town, I don't want to make anyone upset," he finished.

Ah. That was it. Ginny felt better. "It doesn't bother me at all if the job is a week or a month or longer," she assured him. "If you need me, I'd be more than happy to help. If you'd rather have someone else, I will keep an ear out."

"Truthfully," he said, glancing back again at his shop, "I'd like to have you. Maddie has done nothing but talk about you over the last week. I know you hardly met, but she liked you quite a bit."

"I liked her too," Ginny said.

"Then it's settled," Laura said, clapping her hands brightly. "How wonderful!"

"Can you start tomorrow morning?" Josiah asked hopefully.

"Yes. I'll be over bright and early," Ginny said.

"Thank you," Josiah said. He glanced back at his shop. The blacksmith was just opening the door and walking in. "Forgive me, I must go."

He hurried away, and Ginny and Laura watched him.

"How fortunate," Laura said.

"Indeed," Ginny said.

"It is strange, though, that he came all this way to marry a woman and she's nowhere to be found," Laura said, shaking her head. "I feel bad for the man."

"I do too," Ginny said, though that wasn't entirely the truth. She couldn't help it, and scolded herself each time the feeling surfaced, but she couldn't deny that there was something about Josiah that she liked. And she didn't want to think about him getting married.

She stifled a sigh, and hoped Laura wouldn't notice. Luckily, she hadn't. Or, at least, she hadn't shown she did.

"You know as well as I do, though, if she doesn't show up, he won't have any trouble at all finding someone to be his wife. Why, did you see how the single women were looking at him Sunday?"

Ginny didn't answer, but indeed she had. Likely, she'd been one of them.

"I've got to go," Laura said. "Gabriel needed a bit more paper, and I offered to get it from the store. I'll see you later."

Ginny waved, and wandered toward her favorite bench that overlooked the stream. She sat, book in hand, but couldn't seem to concentrate. It was simply because she was about to have a new job, she told herself. Not because she was going to be able to spend more time with Josiah.

A gust of wind fluttered the book's pages in her lap, and as Ginny placed her hand on it to stop them from getting damaged, a fragment of the story caught her attention.

"If she doesn't show up, he might marry me," Rebecca whispered. *"And I think I'd be just fine with that."*

Startled, Ginny let her forefinger trace over the words that were strangely echoing what her heart kept hoping for.

"Me too," Ginny said quietly. "Me too."

Chapter 5

Josiah peeked through the upstairs window of his home, checking for any sign of Ginny. When he didn't see her, he turned back and eyed the room critically. He'd woken earlier than usual, given the place a sound tidying up, and made himself and Maddie a bit of toast with butter and honey for breakfast, then washed the dishes.

He knew that he'd hired Ginny to help with that, but he didn't feel like he could have her start off on the wrong foot. Meaning, with the place a mess.

His eyes sought Maddie, who was sitting at the table, a scowl on her face and her head resting in one hand, elbow on the table. "I don't want to have someone watch after me," she complained. "You said I'd get a new mommy. Where is she?"

"I'd like to know that as well," Josiah said with a small frown, his fingers going to the pocket where he kept the letter. He'd read it frequently, sometimes several times a day, seeking clues as to the woman he was to marry. Last night, frustrated with the entire situation, he'd written a letter of his own to the mail-order marriage agency, asking if there'd been a mistake because he was there, had planned to start his life fresh in Deepwater, and there was no bride.

He planned to see it was delivered to Postmaster Peter that very day to go out in the mail.

"You'll like her," Josiah assured Maddie. "I think."

"Who is it?" Maddie asked. "Not someone old, I hope. I want someone who can play with me. Not scold me all the time if my hands get sticky or I am too noisy."

Her scowl grew, and Josiah held back a sigh. "I'm going downstairs to watch for her," he said. "It shouldn't be much longer."

He hurried down the stairs, unlocked his shop door, and just as he was turning the sign in the window to open, there she came, pink cheeked, a bit of strawberry blonde hair escaping the long braid down her back, and a slightly nervous look on her face.

Somehow, that made Josiah feel a little better. He was nervous too. But she had nothing to fear from him, and he'd be sure she knew that. He couldn't blame her for a little apprehension. After all, he was a stranger. Her reputation was at stake.

The door to his shop opened, and there she stood. With her blew in the breeze, and the faint scent of roses. Josiah wondered if that was from her soap or the flowers potted next door.

"Good morning," Ginny said. "I hope I got here on time?"

"Just perfectly so," Josiah assured her. "I've given Maddie her breakfast. Can I show you around?"

"That would be wonderful," Ginny said. "How are the two of you settling in?"

"I've more business than I could have imagined," Josiah admitted. "That keeps me busy. Maddie, though, she's a little restless. She longs to see things outside the walls of this house."

"Is she allowed to?" Ginny asked. "Tell me what her boundaries are, and I will make sure she doesn't cross them."

"Ah, well," Josiah said slowly, "I admit, I would like her close. For now. I mean, we are new, and..."

He stopped. He couldn't say it. But, to his surprise, Ginny finished just what he'd been thinking.

"And you don't know me," she said frankly. "I don't blame you a bit. Well, let me see," she said, "the café has a collection of books, if you'll allow her to go there. The stream is a popular place for the young ones. I'd make her stay on the bank. There are wildflowers for her to pick, and I could read to her and we could make flower crowns."

She tapped a finger to her lips. "What else? There are always walks, and of course games, which we can do here. Does she have anything in particular she likes to do?"

"She has a doll," Josiah said, "and likes to play tea party with her."

"That's a wonderful game," Ginny agreed. "Shall I go say hello to her?"

"Yes, and I'll show you the kitchen," Josiah said. "If you can see lunch is made for us all, yourself included, and perhaps make dinners. It doesn't have to be fancy at all. Anything, and I'd be grateful. That, and taking care of Maddie, of course."

He pushed open the door at the top of the stairs, and was rewarded with seeing Maddie, still scowling, at the table. But as soon as his daughter saw Ginny, her entire countenance changed, and she jumped up.

"Ginny!"

"Hello, Maddie. I am happy to see you." Ginny gave the girl a warm hug.

"Are you going to look after me while Papa works?" his daughter asked.

"I am! I've so many fun things we can do together. I thought today, perhaps we'd stay here and make cookies and then have a tea party?"

"Oh yes!" Maddie said. "What should we make?"

Josiah slipped from the room, relieved all seemed to be going well. And that Ginny was keeping Maddie nearby.

It wasn't that he didn't trust her. He didn't trust anyone, not really. You never knew what a person was like. He'd learned that well from Celina.

In the front room, Josiah sat at a small worktable and began to cut shirts out of the fabric. He couldn't believe how many orders he had. It was likely he'd need to take on an employee soon. Not that he was complaining one bit about that.

The day passed, and Ginny and Maddie mostly stayed upstairs. They did go outside for a few moments here and there, and twice brought him cookies, and Josiah was surprised at both how quickly the day passed and how much he got done, without needing to stop to help Maddie with this or that. He'd run out quickly to mail his letter to the mail-order agency, but admitted to himself that, with Ginny here, he felt less rushed at the idea of finding a wife.

When he closed his shop at the end of the day and went upstairs, he walked quietly, as he could hear Ginny telling a story.

"...and they all lived happily ever after."

"I will too," Maddie said. "And Papa once we get a new mommy. He needs it."

"You are a sweet girl," Ginny said. She caught sight of him then. "Hello! Is the shop closed?"

"It is," he told her. "I will let you out if you are ready to leave?"

"You will be back, won't you?" Maddie asked, pleadingly.

"Tomorrow morning," Ginny said. "Perhaps your papa won't mind if we visit the café and look at their books?"

He hesitated, then nodded. "That should be fine."

"Then we will do that, and be back for lunch," Ginny said. She leaned over and whispered loudly, "And we will make a pie too."

Maddie clapped her hands, hugged Ginny, and then Ginny followed Josiah down the stairs.

"I can't thank you enough," he said. "Not just for being here, but she looked so happy."

"She's a sweet girl. She deserves to be," Ginny said. In a quieter voice, she added, "Everyone does."

A lump formed in his throat, and he cleared it away. "I agree."

"I'll see you tomorrow," Ginny said, and left through the door he held open.

Josiah didn't answer, instead frozen in place as the scent of roses passed close to him, leaving his heart thumping in the strangest of ways.

Chapter 6

Yawning, Ginny climbed out of her bed and made her way to the window. She'd had yesterday off, Josiah only needing her Monday through Friday. She'd stayed home and helped her mother with things around the house. Today, she'd likely see him and Maddie at church, though she wouldn't be responsible for Maddie until tomorrow.

Another yawn escaped, and Ginny made her way to the basin of water to splash some on her face and tired eyes. She'd had trouble sleeping for the last few nights. At first, she'd been worried that perhaps she was coming down with something. But, when she'd felt fine otherwise, she wondered if she was simply overtired.

Maddie was an energetic little girl. However, Ginny was quite used to being busy and both working hard and thinking up ways to keep children entertained, so she wasn't sure that was it either.

So, what could it be? Was it concern over Maddie and her father? Was that why she couldn't seem to stop thinking about him? Ginny was sure that was it. Just concern over his situation. Nothing more. Certainly not because she'd been thinking about his warm eyes and kind smile, or the way his eyes would sometimes linger on her and fill her with a warm tingly feeling.

Or...maybe it was because, any day, the woman he was to marry may appear. Have an excuse for not being there when he first arrived. He'd marry her, Maddie would have the mother she longed for, and Ginny...Ginny would just go back to the way things had been before Josiah had moved to Deepwater.

She'd be without any chance of a romantic future. No chance of a family all her own, a place to feel loved and wanted and needed.

And she didn't want that. Didn't want him to not need her. Not want her. Even if it wasn't in the way she secretly longed for, Ginny couldn't stand the thought of not seeing him each day.

"Isn't that so silly of me?" she asked her reflection, shaking her head as she pulled her hairbrush through a small tangle. "I shouldn't think that way. I knew when I accepted the job that it was just temporary. He also is to be married. But..."

Her gaze drifted out the window, and in the direction of the town, where she knew Josiah's shop was. "But I want more. I can't help it."

With a heavy sigh that was most unlike her usual cheerful self, Ginny braided her hair, got dressed, helped make breakfast, and joined her family on the walk to church.

The reverend talked that day about continuing on with faith through trials. Ginny listened attentively, thankful that so far in her life, she'd had very few experiences that she could consider a trial. Life was full of uncertainties, Gabriel said, like a forest path that had faded so much you weren't sure which way you should go once you got turned around. That's why it was important to have faith.

Ginny's thoughts wandered. Faith. She had that. But, sometimes it was hard. Like how her mother always told her that her time would come for love and a family. It hadn't yet, and each year that passed, it seemed further away. Her mind flitted back to the idea of becoming a mail-order bride. After seeing firsthand the difficulty that Josiah had with his arranged marriage, she was glad she hadn't done more than consider it.

Josiah.

Why was it that his name came up so often? When she was talking, she always seemed to mention him. When reading, something would spark a thought of him. Even now, in the middle of church, he came to her mind!

Ginny let her gaze roam over those seated in the church. There he was, Maddie by his side. Her breath caught. He looked so handsome in his well-tailored crisp blue shirt and dark pants.

But taken. He was a man who was spoken for, and her thoughts were wrong. It wasn't right to think that way. It also wasn't right for her to feel jealous, especially about the mysterious woman he was to marry, someone she'd never met. Why, the woman might be quite lovely and be a friend. She shouldn't dismiss the idea.

With a sudden start, Ginny realized everyone was standing to sing a closing hymn. She joined in, and then followed the slow procession of people leaving the building.

Just outside, Maddie spotted her and waved. Ginny returned the gesture, and then glanced over as someone grabbed her arm.

"I've hardly seen you," Laura said, linking arms with her. "How has the new job been?"

"It's been wonderful," Ginny said. "A lot of work, but I've enjoyed it, and the pay."

"I'm glad," Laura said. "I love when things work out well."

"Well, I hope they will," Ginny said. She hesitated, then shook her head. "The woman he was to marry still hasn't shown herself or written him."

Laura looked thoughtful. "Perhaps it's not meant for him to be with her," she said. "It might be God has other plans for him. And for her."

"I'm sure you are right," Ginny said. She didn't look at her friend. She was worried that Laura, who was incredibly perceptive, might see that she was hoping the other woman never appeared. That one day, Josiah might look at her with interest.

"It's a difficult situation," Laura continued. "We had Josiah and Maddie over for dinner last night. He seems troubled, but not like a man who is worried about his bride's safety."

"What do you mean?" Ginny asked.

"He seemed almost..." she paused, seeming to search for the right words, "relieved she'd not shown up." Laura glanced sideways at Ginny. "Your name was mentioned several times. By him and his daughter."

Ginny hoped she wasn't blushing. "Oh?" she asked, trying not to sound too interested, though she was.

"Yes," Laura said. She squeezed Ginny's hand. "I need to go speak with someone," she said, "but, I just wanted to let you know that I've been praying."

"For what?" Ginny asked.

The reverend's wife smiled. "For your happiness," she answered. "And, perhaps, that you become his bride. I think the two of you are well suited."

Ginny's jaw dropped, but before she could say anything, Laura had vanished.

Chapter 7

"What do you think?" Josiah asked, watching as Hank turned himself this way and that, then ran his hands along the front of the fawn-brown shirt.

"I think I better not tell Maggie this is the best-fitting shirt and trousers I've ever had. She might not cook me dinner," Hank said, shaking his head. He let out a low whistle. "You sure do fine work. Can I get two more shirts, one cream and one blue, and another pair of dark trousers?"

"Of course," Josiah said, writing the order down on his notepad. "It will be about three weeks."

"I'd wait longer, if needed," Hank said. "You just send word when they are ready. I'll just wear these now, and carry out my old ones." He reached for his old pants and pulled out some money from the pocket. "Are you finding you keep busy here?"

"I am," Josiah agreed, taking the payment and putting it in his cash box. "I've had near half the town come in, it seems."

"That's because as busy as we all are, it's nice to have a tailor here. I know Maggie is relieved. She works so hard in the café, it was difficult for her to make my clothes and hers. That's why the moment you opened shop, she told me to place my order. We'll be bringing our son around to you soon for a few things for him."

"I'll be glad to fit him," Josiah said, meaning every word. He was still amazed at how quickly his business had flourished. No doubt, it was helpful not having competition from others in the same capacity, but he really was surprised at how readily everyone had accepted him, and his tailoring.

His door opened, and Dirk, the original owner of his building and the town's printer, strode in with a grin. "I'm here for my fitting," he said. Then he raised his eyebrows. "Did you just get those made?" He studied Hank, and walked around him slowly.

"Sure did. Have more on order," Hank said proudly.

"Then I'd better hurry to get my own order put in," Dirk said. "Won't be long before anyone who hasn't been here is, and you are backed up for weeks. Months."

Josiah chuckled, "From your mouth to God's ears," he said. "I enjoy being busy, and a little to set by for a rainy day is always welcome."

"You'll have that and more. I'll see you later," Hank said, waving as he took his leave.

"Let me get my tape measure," Josiah said, "if you'll step this way?"

He led Dirk to the small back room he had reserved for his customers to try on their garments or to be fitted. "Now, can you loosen your collar? I want to fit you properly, and then arms out," he said, and began to take Dirk's measurements, scribbling them down on his small notebook. Tonight, he'd write them again in a larger book that he planned to keep so that frequent customers could have their garments made without delay, if they didn't feel they had grown in one direction or another.

"Heard you're waiting for your wife to join you," Dirk commented.

"Yes," Josiah said. "It's a...strange situation."

"So I hear," Dirk said. "I hope I didn't offend you, though, by my asking. I didn't mean anything by it. Just curious. Everyone likes to welcome a new person."

"Not at all," Josiah said. "Though, if I'm being truthful, since she wasn't here and I have settled in, I'm not sure I need a wife anymore. I have Ginny."

"She's a good one," Dirk said. "Say, if the other woman doesn't show up, why don't you marry her?"

Josiah dropped his pencil and grabbed for it. As his fingers reached it, he nervously knocked it again, and it rolled away. "Ah, Ginny," he said, fumbling for the pencil. "Well, she is just here to help. Temporarily."

"To care for your daughter and cook, isn't it?" Dirk asked.

"That's right." Josiah wasn't sure why he felt so nervous. Was it because of the idea of him marrying Ginny? He'd never admit how he'd thought about that more than once, but he was also more than aware of the fact that a beautiful woman like that, one who was full of smiles and laughter, would want nothing to do with a man like him. Somber and boring. He was but a simple tailor. A man such as he would never catch the eye of someone so lovely. He was sure that Ginny must have a half dozen men interested in her hand.

"So, why not marry her? You'd at least know what you are getting," Dirk said, shrugging his shirt back where it had slipped, and fastening the buttons.

"Well, that is..." Josiah stopped. What Dirk was saying had reason behind it. There was no need for the man to know he'd already thought of such a thing. And just as quickly had dismissed it. There was no way at all she'd even consider it, nor would he ask.

"I understand," Dirk said, looking at him sympathetically. "You're a man of your word. Trying to do the right thing and wait for the woman you agreed to marry."

"That's right," Josiah said quickly. "It wouldn't be proper of me to leave her high and dry." Then, he wryly added, "Even if that's what I'm feeling happened to me. I'm trying to be mindful of the fact something might have happened to delay her, and hopefully I'll hear from the agency who sent me here. I mailed a letter quite some time ago and thought I'd have a reply by now."

"Well, I'm sure it's all going to work out for you," Dirk said as he walked to the front of the store. "Things have a way of doing that here in Deepwater."

"So I've heard," Josiah said. And it was true. He could hardly believe all the lives that had changed—for the better—all because of this town. The town had brought together those who were in need of something, and it had been provided in one way or another. Perhaps that would happen for him.

That said, Josiah wasn't sure what he needed. It wasn't a wife. He knew that because he'd managed fine without one for years. But it was true something felt missing in his life. Could Deepwater help him? He didn't have a past like the reverend, or a secret like Alyssa had, and he wasn't trying to leave heartache like Dirk, or run from a scandal like his wife, Samantha, but...well, actually, maybe he was.

Maybe he had all of those things. His bleak, hurtful past, the heartache that seemed to follow him from place to place, and while, as far as he knew, there was no scandal lurking about other than the fact he'd been so undesirable his wife had left him, a terrible thought formed.

Ginny was unmarried, quite eligible, and beautiful. She was sweet and caring and...what if someone got the wrong idea about them? Or what if she had a beau and the man was the jealous sort? A cold chill went through him just then. He realized that these last few weeks they'd settled into a comfortable routine. He enjoyed Ginny being around, and her smiles that made him smile, her somehow always knowing right when he was hungry or thirsty, her thoughtful care with his daughter who absolutely adored her. It was obvious that Maddie had formed a connection with her.

It was going to greatly upset Madeline when his promised wife did eventually come and Ginny left. He wasn't looking forward to that day, for more reasons than one.

"See you later," Dirk said, glancing over the notepad where Josiah had been writing down his order while simultaneously thinking about his difficult situation. "I can't wait to see my new shirts."

"They'll be ready as soon as possible. Have a good day," Josiah said.

As he turned back to his workbench, his eyes caught sight of Ginny and Maddie outside of the window. Each held a book in their hands, and must have been coming from the café's library.

His chest felt tight at the sight of her, and he couldn't seem to look away. Each day that the woman he was to marry didn't show was one day more he had with Ginny. He'd had so many now, imagining life without her was quite difficult. He didn't want to be married to the other woman, but he had no choice. Though Dirk didn't know him well, nor Josiah him, the man was right about one thing. Josiah was a man of his word. He'd agreed to marry a particular woman, and that's what he planned to do.

When she did arrive, Josiah knew it would break his heart, even if Ginny had no idea he harbored a secret affection for her.

And that's just how it would be. She'd never know. Because he was never going to give his heart away again. Hence the marriage of convenience. It was the only way to avoid the pain that would inevitably come.

Chapter 8

"It's so pretty!" Maddie's voice was hushed as she looked at the tiny shawl Ginny had knitted for her doll. What Maddie didn't know was that Ginny had been working on a larger, identical one for Maddie.

"I can help you to make more clothes for your doll," Ginny said. "You already can make basic stitches. Together, we can work on some things for her. Why don't we try to make her a dress this week? I have some scrap fabric that would be the perfect size. It's a sunny yellow, with some little roses on it."

"You'd help me?" Maddie asked.

"Of course," Ginny said. When her charge was quiet for a long moment, Ginny softly asked, "Are you okay?"

"I always wanted a mama to do that with me," Maddie said quietly. Then she looked up, and Ginny saw the little girl's chin quiver and heard the tears in her voice. "Don't tell Papa, please. I don't want him to feel bad. He's a good papa and does a lot already."

"I won't, dear," Ginny promised.

She felt terrible for Maddie. It had been obvious to her from early on that the little girl needed the affection and attention only a woman could give her. She eagerly learned everything Ginny taught her, and followed her about willingly. When Ginny sat, Maddie would sit right next to her, as close as she could.

"I wonder if my old mama would have done this," Maddie said wistfully, as she fastened the shawl on the doll. "Make me something pretty."

"I'm sure she would have," Ginny assured her. "I'm also sure she loved you very much."

"That's not true," Maddie said, shaking her head. "If it was, she wouldn't have left us."

"Well, sometimes we don't get a choice when someone leaves us," Ginny said slowly, wondering how much about death the small girl knew. Explaining the loss of a loved one wasn't something she had experience in doing.

Before she could say more, Maddie made a huffing sound. "Still. I wish she'd have at least written. Said goodbye or that she loved me. Mrs. Martin, the lady who used to watch me, said my mama was pretty, but she was spoiled. That's why she ran away when I was just a few days old."

Ginny stilled. "Ran away?"

"Yes. I wonder if she got lost. And that's why she didn't come back." Maddie shrugged. "Papa doesn't like to talk about it. But..." her voice grew wistful again, "but sometimes I want to be like everyone else and have a mama." Her face lit up then. "Maybe that's why we're here, still waiting. Maybe my new mama is my old mama! Our family will get fixed again. I bet that's it!"

"I...I don't know," Ginny said. This conversation wasn't going in a direction she felt comfortable with. She hadn't realized Maddie's mother had left them. She had just assumed she'd passed away. It happened. However, Maddie had some serious questions, and she needed to let Josiah know. Especially if she was working herself up to think her mother was returning. Until she could speak with him, she'd best distract her.

Going over to her basket she'd brought with her, Ginny pulled out some sheets of paper and a freshly sharpened pencil. "Would you like to draw your papa a picture?" she asked. "Perhaps he will hang it in his shop somewhere."

"Yes!" Maddie said, and plopped into one of the chairs at the table.

"You start. I'll take him a bit of lunch," Ginny said, "and then you and I can have ours."

"Uh-huh," Maddie said, already focused on her picture and not really hearing her.

Ginny picked up the plate with bread, a slice of ham, a wedge of cheese, and an apple, then carried it down the stairs and into the shop. She couldn't hear Josiah talking to anyone, so hoped that he was alone. If he was, she wanted to tell him what Maddie had said, before too much time had passed.

She found him sitting at his workbench, carefully cutting a shirt out of a light blue fabric. He looked up and smiled at her as she approached.

"Thank you," he said. "I appreciate this. I was starting to get hungry."

"Then I'm just in time," she said with a small laugh.

"You spoil me with all you do," Josiah said. "That's something I'm not used to, but I'm so appreciative."

Ginny flushed in pleasure. But then uncertainty came over her. She had to tell him. Broach the subject. "Have you...a moment?" she asked.

"Of course." He set down his scissors and looked at her, concern in his dark eyes. "Is something wrong?"

Ginny lowered her voice, as she sat in the other chair at his worktable. "Maddie has been talking about her mother."

He didn't say anything for a moment, but dropped his head into his hands. After a deep sigh, he looked up and asked, "The woman I'm waiting for? Or her real mother?"

"Her real one," Ginny said. "She...she seems to have just now convinced herself that the woman who you are to marry might be her real mother. She thinks, perhaps, her mother left one day and got lost, and that's why she doesn't have her."

Josiah swallowed hard, and shook his head. "This is my fault for talking so little about her," he said. "But how does one tell a child their mother left them? It would make her feel unloved."

"I feel terrible for telling you this," Ginny said. "It just felt like something I should let you know."

"I appreciate it," he sighed. "I'm sure you have questions too. Here, I've asked you into my home, asked you to care for my child, and you know nothing of the wounds she bears."

"Do you bear them as well?" Ginny asked, studying him.

To her surprise, he didn't look away, but met her eyes. "I do. No matter where I go, no matter what I do, thoughts of Celina find me. Even though she left me, I can't seem to leave her."

Ginny wanted to ask what happened, even if it would be rude. But the pain in his voice and on his face stopped her. It was obvious that he was suffering, and had been for years. She started to stand. "I'm sorry. It's none of my business. I feel terrible for even saying anything."

As she turned to go, a movement stopped her. Ginny looked down. Josiah's hand was on her arm. "Don't go," he told her. "I want...I want to tell you."

She turned back to him. "Are you sure?"

"Yes. No. It is a story I do not enjoy. But I need to. I want you to understand."

Ginny nodded. When he removed his hand, she sat back down, but touched the spot his hand had been on moments before. Goosebumps filled her, and she hoped that he wouldn't notice.

"Celina and I were young. Too young to marry," he began, pacing for a moment. "But we were in love. I thought. Right after we were married, I learned she'd only chosen me because she'd been caught in a compromising situation with another man. The one she'd wanted to marry, but her parents had said no. A marriage to me would stop any potential talk. Just under a year later, we welcomed Maddie into our lives. But all during the time she was with child, Celina was distant. Angry. She talked about how much she regretted her life.

"When Maddie was born, I'd hoped seeing our daughter, so tiny and perfect, would bring Celina some joy. But it didn't. Maddie was not even a week old when Celina left. There was no goodbye. Simply a note saying she wasn't coming back. There was no apology. No words of love. We stayed in that house until we moved here, and she never sent word. Not once."

Josiah sat, and buried his head in his hands again. "I have accepted that she didn't love me. But it pains me that our child wasn't enough to keep her with us. I feel badly that I let Celina down, that I was not who she wanted, but I feel worse that I let Maddie down, by not providing enough for her mother to keep her content."

Ginny felt shocked. "You can't think any of that was your fault," she said.

"But I do." He looked up at her then, and the sad smile he gave her made her heart ache. "It is obvious that I do not possess the ability to be a good husband. It was with great hesitation that I petitioned for a divorce, on grounds of desertion. That way I could legally remarry so that Maddie could have someone to care for her. And that's also why this marriage of convenience is going to be, well, convenient. Maddie will get what she needs, and the woman will know upfront what I can give her. Then, if she accepts, there will be no disappointment on her end, and Maddie's heart will also be shielded."

Ginny felt like she was having trouble breathing. This was worse than she'd thought. Both he and Maddie had been hurt so terribly, but whereas Maddie was young, and had a chance for her pain to dissipate, Josiah's had not, and worse, he blamed himself for his wife's departure. To the point that he had given up on love.

"I've done the best that I can," Josiah said, "but a father alone is not enough."

"You've done a wonderful job," Ginny said, reaching over and resting her hand on his before she realized what she was doing. "Maddie is sweet and kind, well behaved and clever. You should be proud of yourself and her."

His other hand rested on top of hers, and Ginny felt slightly dizzy from the intimate contact. She couldn't recall anyone ever touching her like that. If they had, it certainly hadn't affected her in that way.

"I'm so grateful for you, Ginny," he said.

She adored the sound of her name on his lips. Ginny wanted to speak, but her tongue felt frozen, and she was having difficulty thinking. Her attraction to him had only grown, and it was near to the point that he was on her mind constantly.

"I wouldn't know what to do without you," he added, his voice low.

A shiver ran through Ginny, and she whispered, "I'm yours, for as long as you want me."

"There is...no one waiting for you?" he asked, both a surprise and a hesitation in his voice.

"No," Ginny whispered.

The air grew heavy with something unsaid, and Ginny could tell Josiah felt it too. The meaning behind her words and his could have been platonic. They could have been referring to her minding Maddie, to helping cook. But they also could have meant so, so much more.

How she'd be his, heart and soul, if he asked. How she'd stay, forever, if he wanted her to, even if it was just like this. Not an object of his affection, but simply nearby.

Would he say anything? If he did, how would she react? Especially if it wasn't the thing she longed to hear? She knew he was waiting for his wife-to-be. She shouldn't even hope or wish that he'd notice her, be in love with her, but Ginny couldn't stop herself.

"Ginny." His voice was low, filled with something she couldn't describe, but knew she wanted more of. Josiah leaned just a little closer, and she nearly stopped breathing. Was he about to kiss her?

The shop door opened just then, and Josiah jerked away and stood, going to the customer. Slightly shaken, Ginny slipped back upstairs to get Maddie her lunch. Her heart was thumping so loudly she could feel it in her ears.

Before she went into the room with Maddie, Ginny closed her eyes. She'd made a terrible mistake, falling for a man who didn't desire anything more than a wife of convenience. She knew it was to protect his heart, but somehow, she'd lost hers to him, and knew that after he'd held her hand, she'd never be the same.

Chapter 9

Josiah felt as though his eyes were filled with grit. They were dry, aching, and every inch of him was exhausted. But he guessed after not sleeping for a few nights, that was pretty normal. He wished, almost, that he had an illness. An injury. Some reason to blame on his inability to fall asleep and stay asleep, but he had none.

Well, that wasn't true. He had a reason. Her name was Ginny. Ginny with the sweet face and soft skin, whose hand fit so perfectly in his. Who made him feel lightheaded and funny in his stomach and tense and awkward and a million other things.

Worse, was he remembered the first time he'd felt all those things. With Celina. When he'd fallen for her. And he couldn't fall for Ginny. It was a bad idea. The worst ever.

First, there was her reputation to think of. Then, there was his. People were prone to gossip, and he was sure even in Deepwater, where everyone seemed kind, that any sort of indiscretion or appearance of an indiscretion would be known almost immediately.

He couldn't do that to her. Couldn't do that to himself. After all, he had Maddie to think about. And the woman he'd come to marry, even if she hadn't made herself known.

So, what had he been thinking, as he covered Ginny's hand with his own? Asking her if she had anyone...Time had almost stopped, and he'd felt a heavy pull toward her. In fact, he realized he'd been leaning close to her. His eyes had been focused on one thing. Her lips.

Josiah dragged his fingers through his hair. What was wrong with him? Going around, acting all moon-faced over a woman. He knew better than this. That's why it upset him so much. Made him unable to function properly, and that was no way at all to run a business.

He wasn't acting smart. Wasn't looking out for himself and Maddie like he had the last six years. Josiah drew in a shaky breath, pushed back his shoulders, and faced the man he saw in the mirror's reflection. "Pull yourself together," he said sternly. "Love isn't for you. Love isn't even real. It's a fleeting emotion that fades. Now, on to work. That's real. Tangible. Reliable."

And for the next three hours, that's just what he did. Worked as hard as he could cutting fabric, sewing shirts, taking orders, and smiling at his customers even if he didn't feel the least bit like it.

It was nearing noon, and Josiah could hear Ginny on the stairs. He couldn't do it. Couldn't face her right now. Quickly, he strode to the shop door, just as she appeared with a bowl of something that steamed from it.

"I have your lunch," she said with a smile. "Unless you'd rather eat upstairs today?"

"I've got to run over to the post office," Josiah said. "I'll eat when I get back, if you just want to leave it."

"Oh, of course," Ginny said, with a faltering smile.

It nearly did him in. Without waiting any longer, Josiah hurried over to the post office. He didn't need to go, but he had been each day the mail arrived, just like the others in Deepwater did. To see if he had anything.

As he waited in the short line, Josiah tried not to feel impatient. Perhaps today would be the day he received a letter from the mail-order agency. He hoped so. He was tired of waiting. The waiting made him anxious and worried. For both his future and Maddie's.

At last, it was his turn, and Josiah stepped to the counter. "Ah! Letter for you," Peter said, reaching into a slot where the mail was neatly sorted. "Here you go."

Josiah took it, and his heart leaped as he looked at the sender. It was from the agency! At last! A quick glance over his shoulder showed no one waiting, and Josiah tore open the letter and skimmed it, not wanting to waste another moment. As he read the words and his mind started to absorb them, his stomach started to churn.

"You're looking a little green around the edges," Peter said, as he walked past the window. "Don't mean to pry, but bad news?"

"I'm...I'm not sure," Josiah admitted. "This says that there was a delay, but she'll be here soon."

"Who's that?" Peter asked. "The woman you were to marry?"

"Maybe? I don't know. Truthfully, I was never told the woman's name, and it's not in this letter. My previous letter only said that she was waiting and I'd find her at the café. Which, as you and I bet everyone else here knows, didn't happen." Josiah looked at the letter in his hands. "I don't know just what to think."

"I'm sure it will all be sorted soon, and rightly," Peter said, trying to reassure him. "Sometimes our minds play tricks on us, and make a situation seem worse than it is. Mark my words, once she arrives you'll be feeling much better, and the whole thing will be straightened out easily."

A woman stepped up behind Josiah then, and he moved away so she could get her mail. He wished that he had Peter's confidence. And he also wished that yes, it would all be sorted out swiftly. There was too much of the unknown, too much uncertainty around the entire situation.

Josiah wondered, and not for the first time, if he'd made a mistake uprooting Maddie and coming here. Deepwater was a beautiful town, full of welcoming individuals, but it hadn't brought the peace he'd hoped for. Not yet, anyway. Perhaps once the woman arrived, and they decided if they were to wed or not, he could put the past behind him and fully embrace the present and future. Until then, he had to remember that he was a man with an intended. He needed to act like it.

Slowly, Josiah returned to his shop, the letter in his pocket feeling as though it weighed as much as a brick. He pushed open the door, and spotted the lunch Ginny had thoughtfully made him. It was still warm. But the lump in his stomach wouldn't let him eat. He felt sick, even thinking about it.

He could hear footsteps above him, and laughter. Swallowing hard, Josiah imagined Maddie and Ginny playing some sort of game. They both looked happy, their eyes shining brightly. He wondered what would happen if Ginny turned that gaze to him. If they had a moment alone where he could profess the confusion he felt, and the conflict of wanting to get to know her better, the need to distance himself. Would she understand? He doubted it.

Josiah shook his head. A beautiful woman like that. She likely had suitors knocking down her door, even if she claimed otherwise. It didn't matter he'd never seen her with one. He also hadn't been around her outside of his shop, mindful of appearances. The only other time he saw her was in church, and she sat with her family, and he left quickly afterward. She had a whole other life—had it before he'd even arrived—and he knew nothing about it. He'd fallen in love—there, he'd said it—with the Ginny he saw each day. Not the Ginny who really was.

Were they one and the same? Was anyone? There wasn't an answer to that, and puzzling it in his mind made his head ache and his stomach churn worse.

What would happen when this other woman came? Would he turn her away? Perhaps she would refuse him. That would, in a sense, make things easier for him. But if she did, would his wounded pride let him pursue Ginny? It was doubtful. As Celina was fond of telling him, no woman would willingly marry a tailor and expect a life more than drudgery.

Pain seeped through his every pore, and Josiah fought back the anger and hurt that always followed. Why? Why couldn't he ever forget? Move forward?

Trying to distance himself from his tormented thoughts the only way he knew how, Josiah bent over a shirt, sewing on the buttons. If he could lose himself, even for an hour in his work, let the ache ease just a little, he'd consider that a blessing.

Chapter 10

An unease filled the small house when Josiah came upstairs at the end of the day. He hugged Maddie and listened to her tell him about the cake they'd made as a surprise for him and how they'd picked berries in the forest's nearby blackberry bushes, but Ginny could tell his mind wasn't really focusing on what his daughter was saying.

For some reason, she was quite worried about that. And him. Ginny tried to keep her tone light and act as though she couldn't feel his distance as she told Maddie goodbye, but as she followed a silent Josiah down the stairs, it was almost crushing how heavy the quiet was.

"Forgive me for asking, but I sense something amiss. Are you...are you feeling well?" Ginny ventured, hesitating as they neared the door.

"As well as can be expected," he answered with a tight smile. "Have a good weekend."

She stopped, standing partway in the open door. "Josiah, if you need someone to talk to ever...I mean, if I can help somehow..." Ginny didn't know what to say or if she should even say anything. She bit her lip, and stood there feeling like a fool.

"You cannot," he told her, with that same tight smile, "but I thank you for all you've been doing to look after Maddie and help with the meals. She enjoys having you around. Have a good weekend."

Ginny nodded, and left quickly before Josiah could see the hurt on her face. He'd said Maddie enjoyed having her around. Not us, not we, not I. Maddie.

She didn't know what had happened, but today he had been so cold and distant to her. Why? She hadn't done anything out of the ordinary. Every one of his wishes about keeping his daughter close by had been obeyed, and without fail, Ginny had lunch and dinners made, and even helped with the housework. Until today, he'd been so appreciative, so kind.

As she walked home, Ginny's mind spun around every interaction they'd had over the last few days. It had all been normal. Until he had told her about his wife. Was that it? He was upset? Embarrassed? It had obviously been a very difficult story to tell, and far worse to have lived and then share with others. But he hadn't seemed distressed in that way. Everything had been just fine. Why, he'd...

He'd held her hand.

The air had nearly crackled with energy. Ginny had wondered if more might happen. Then, someone had come in and he'd jerked away.

Ginny felt hot tears roll down her cheeks. That was it. It had to be. He was ashamed to be so near her and her wanton behavior. She'd instigated it, by reaching out and touching him. What must he think of her? It was obvious he blamed her for an indiscretion. And how could she have been so foolish? She knew better! He was a man with an intended. And she...she had forgotten that for a moment.

No wonder he was upset. He was trying to keep a proper distance, without hurting her feelings. Without telling her how in the wrong she'd been. She worked for him, nothing more. That was, if he kept her on. She might have to find something else, to continue to save for the future she was sure she'd be alone in.

Ginny sniffled, and wiped at her eyes with her handkerchief. She was so ashamed. She was also grateful that she'd go two days without seeing him. It would give her time to think. Perhaps she should stop working for him now. Tell him to make other arrangements. She'd have to leave one day anyway, when his intended arrived. Why not sooner than later? Hide from her shame? He was a good man. Surely he'd never tell anyone how she'd acted.

Josiah was nothing but kind. Too kind. He didn't dare speak of it to her, and that made things feel worse. She should have known that the moment they shared meant nothing to anyone but her.

Her house rose ahead of her, and Ginny quickly wiped one last tear from her face, hoping no one would notice how upset she was when she walked inside. Last Friday, she couldn't wait for Monday to come to return to Josiah and Maddie. Now, she hoped it never did.

Chapter 11

Saturday had dragged on slower than Josiah could have imagined. He'd been hesitant to tell Maddie that her potential mother was arriving, but when he had moved through the house with a near fury, trying to scrub the already-clean kitchen and bedrooms to make his best impression, she'd guessed, somehow, and had gotten very excited.

In a way, that was good. Maddie went to choose an outfit for herself and her doll. With that small reprieve, he didn't have to hide his anxiousness. There had been no questions about Ginny from her to plague his mind. Usually, Maddie chattered most of the weekend away about Ginny. That used to not be something he minded.

But that was before everything had changed, and that was not something that he could handle right now. Not after it had taken all he had in him to send her on her way the day before, instead of doing what he'd longed to, and that was pulling her into his arms and asking her to marry him, and dismissing the woman who'd kept him waiting and wondering where and who she was.

Now, the house scrubbed and nothing to do, Josiah split his attention between Maddie and working on his order for Hank. But it was no good. He was restless in a way where he knew he'd make mistakes and simply cause himself to do more work or worse, ruin the fabric. Suddenly, he sprang from his chair. "Maddie," he called. "Let's go for a walk."

That sounded good. Something to clear his mind. Distract his pained heart and the fears that were filling him. Maybe even get the image of Ginny out of his mind, and her eyes that had been brimming with tears. How he loathed himself for causing her sorrow. That was all he was good for with women, wasn't it?

In short order, Maddie was alongside him and they wandered through Deepwater as he tried to leave his troubles behind. First, to Maggie's Café for a cookie and a hand pie. Josiah also ordered one of Carissa's cherry cheese pies to pick up on Monday. He'd heard so much about them, he was eager to try one for himself. Then, they strolled up one side of the town, then the other, soon finding themselves on the small path that led near the church.

Josiah wasn't sure why he went there, other than he knew there was a garden area with benches and it felt restful. Peaceful. And that was something he was in sore need of right now.

They walked among the late summer roses and pansies and some other flowers that Josiah couldn't name but agreed with Maddie they were pretty. He sat on a bench and watched as Maddie chased a butterfly, and then started to chatter away to her doll, just on the other side of a large lilac bush that was starting to fade.

Then, at the sound of a man's chuckle, he shot up from his seat as he realized she wasn't talking to her doll, but to a person. Fear for his daughter's safety coursed through him, and he nearly ran around the bush, only to find the reverend and his wife smiling at him.

"Josiah," Gabriel said warmly. "How are you? Maddie was just telling us the news that your wife will be arriving."

He nodded, relaxing now that he knew who was there. "I think so, anyway. And then we will see if we are suited." He smiled at Maddie, though it felt forced. "She must also agree to the marriage. Perhaps she won't want me."

"Oh, Papa," Maddie said, shaking her head. "Who wouldn't love you? I know Ginny does!"

Josiah was sure his face was a crimson color. Laura, though, smoothly said, "Josiah, might I take Maddie around to the schoolhouse to show it to her? Soon, she'll be there, and I think she might feel more at ease seeing it beforehand."

That was right. Laura was also the teacher here in Deepwater. What she said made sense, and he welcomed the distraction she offered from his embarrassment, bless her.

"Yes, that would be fine," he stammered, and watched as Maddie skipped along with Laura. They went in the direction of the school, which he could see from where he stood.

"I sense something bothering you, my friend," Gabriel said quietly, touching his shoulder briefly. "Would you like to talk about it?"

Josiah considered the question. He knew that Gabriel wouldn't force him to speak if he didn't want to. But, he also, while not having experienced it firsthand, knew the man was very wise and a source of good advice. That was something he was in need of right now. And, as he already knew a good deal about Josiah's situation, what was the harm?

He mulled the decision over in his mind for a moment before he nodded. "I am struggling with the idea of remarriage," Josiah finally said, slowly.

Instead of reassuring him, like everyone else had seemed to do, Gabriel nodded slowly. "I would imagine so," he said. "There's much to think about."

There was quiet for a moment, and Josiah stared toward the schoolhouse, letting every bit of his sadness come to the surface. "I don't want to make another mistake."

"Was your first marriage a mistake?" Gabriel asked. "Or was it just part of life?" He added, before Josiah could answer, "After all, you have your beautiful, clever daughter. She is a joy to be around, and without that marriage, you wouldn't have her."

"You are right," Josiah said. "She's...that's not what I meant by a mistake. But now that I have her, I want to protect her."

"That's a father's instinct." Gabriel nodded. "Though I've no children of my own, yet, I feel that same protectiveness of everyone here in Deepwater. But I also know that things happen in life that we don't always enjoy. They are painful and difficult to get through or to get over because they are preparing us for something else. Something better. Perhaps, even something that we wouldn't be ready for or appreciate, without going through such a difficult thing first."

"But what am I to do?" Josiah whispered. "How do I make this fear, this great unease go away?"

"I'm not sure if any of us will ever be without such a thing," Gabriel said, thoughtfully. "It often appears when we feel helpless in a situation."

"Which is how I am feeling right now," Josiah admitted.

"We can't control everything, my friend," Gabriel said. "But I do know there are more good people than not, and not everyone who wants to get close to you is out to harm you."

Ginny's face appeared in his mind, and guilt filled him. She'd asked for nothing. Had only offered herself and her time. Had cared for and loved his child. Him.

But then, his heart hardened. It was what he had to do, what he'd always had to do, to protect his daughter. To protect himself. That was why he'd come to Deepwater. Why he'd agreed to a mail-order match.

"No, I don't think everyone is," he finally answered Gabriel.

"Perhaps you only feel that way about the female variety," the reverend answered, raising his brows.

"That's different," Josiah answered.

And it was. Because if he'd learned anything, it was that the human heart was fragile, and once it had been bruised, betrayed, or shattered, it was impossible to repair.

Chapter 12

Though Maddie had nearly floated through the air that day with her excitement of having a mother at last, Josiah was a stark contrast. When he spoke, it was terse, his posture was tense, and more than once, Ginny spotted him with his head in his hands.

Truthfully, she felt like doing just the same. And could anyone blame her? A woman was coming today to marry the man she'd somehow fallen for. It didn't matter he didn't know it, it hurt all the same. The night before, Ginny had practiced her smile. The one that said everything was just fine and she was happy for him. But no matter how much she tried, it never met her eyes.

When she'd arrived yesterday to start the week with Josiah, he'd told her the news. Maddie was thrilled, and talked nonstop about her soon-to-be mother, but it had taken almost everything in Ginny not to run back home, climb into her bed, and hide so she could cry.

"Is the cake done?" Maddie asked, coming into the kitchen. Ginny saw she'd changed her dress again, likely hoping to make a good first impression on the woman her father was to marry.

"I'm checking it now," Ginny promised, and peeked into the oven. The color looked good, and the smell was even better. This cake was one she could make almost with her eyes shut, and knew anyone who ate it would love it. "Yes." Ginny reached for a kitchen towel. "Let me pull it out. Stand back."

Maddie did as she was instructed, and Ginny took the poundcake out of the oven, setting the hot pan onto a second kitchen towel so that it could cool.

"It looks yummy," Maddie said, breathing in deeply.

"You've become a fine baker, little miss," Ginny said with a smile to the girl. She'd miss her once she was no longer needed. It was likely Maddie hadn't realized Ginny wouldn't still be there, not once she had a mother who would want to run things her own way. However, neither she, nor, to her knowledge, Josiah had told her as such. The idea of doing so brought tears to Ginny's eyes each time.

Suppressing a sigh and pushing her sad feelings down, Ginny closed the oven door and stirred the potato and carrot stew. The woman wouldn't want to cook her first evening there, of that Ginny was sure.

She kept herself busy while Maddie ran from window to window, looking for the stage. When slow, heavy footsteps sounded on the stairs, Ginny turned, knowing it was time.

"Let's meet the stage," Josiah said, without any enthusiasm in his voice.

For some reason, his tone made Ginny feel slightly better. It was as though he was as reluctant as she was. Ginny didn't want to meet the woman who would take her place, but Maddie had wanted her there, and Josiah hadn't said anything to the contrary, so she was joining them.

Maddie ran down the stairs before him, and Ginny slowly went afterward. Partway on the stairs, Josiah stopped, and looked at her. "I'm sorry," he said.

"For what?" Ginny asked, shaking her head.

He searched her face for a long moment, then said, his voice so quiet she could hardly hear him, "I wish things were different."

Ginny's heart sped up. Was Josiah trying to tell her something? That, perhaps, he regretted the idea of marriage to the woman who was arriving? Even was interested in her? A tiny spark of hope formed. She could hardly breathe she was so hopeful. Would he say more? Encourage her to say something? Might he even tell her that he wasn't going to marry the woman?

Ginny longed to beg him to say what was really on his heart. But she couldn't. That wouldn't have been proper. Perhaps she didn't even want to know. After all, she might not like whatever he said. So, instead, she followed him as he turned and continued down the stairs, and went outside on the short walk to the stage stop.

The entire walk, she berated herself. How could she keep thinking and hoping for his affection? What was wrong with her? She needed to stop thinking that way. He was about to be married. And if her future was to be that of a woman alone, as she'd been so far, her traitorous thoughts of longing for Josiah would serve to do nothing but cause her pain.

Hadn't she already suffered enough of that over the years, feeling unloved and unwanted? She didn't need more.

Ginny glanced at Josiah, with his stoic expression, and Maddie, who was all smiles and nearly skipping along. What a contrast they were. And then there she was, almost in tears. What would the woman think of them?

They'd just arrived when Maddie shrieked, "There it is!" and pointed to the cloud of dust in the distance.

There it was indeed.

Silently, she and Josiah waited as the stage pulled up and the driver hopped down. Maddie had been twitching, nearly bursting with excitement. It was all the young girl could do not to race over to the stage. Had her father's hand not been on her shoulder, Ginny suspected she might have.

For herself, she couldn't take her eyes off of the stage. Each moment felt torturous. Finally, the driver opened the door to the stage. However, no one got out. In fact, she could see now through the small windows that the interior was empty. Ginny felt confused, and looked at Josiah, who appeared much the same.

"Excuse me," Josiah called to the driver. "Was no one on the stage? Did someone miss it, perhaps? A woman?"

"No, sir," the driver answered, as he closed the door behind the woman who entered the stagecoach. "Had no one scheduled."

"But..." Josiah frowned, not finishing what he had started to say.

The horses were quickly changed and the passenger's bag secured. Immediately, the stage left, dust rising once more in a cloud in the street, but Ginny, Josiah, and Maddie stood, glancing around as if the driver might be wrong and his future wife would appear.

"Where's Mama?" Maddie asked, tugging her father's arm. "Why isn't she here?"

"I don't know." Josiah's face was as dark as a storm cloud.

"Perhaps there's a note from her?" Ginny suggested. "The driver did speak to Hank when he changed the horses."

Josiah shook his head. His jaw was set, and a muscle twitched. "It really doesn't matter at this point. I came here because of her. When she said she was delayed, I waited, patiently. Now, I'm here and again she is not. I'm tired of whatever game she is playing. It's not right, and it's not fair to Maddie."

"It's not fair to you either, Papa," Maddie said, her wide eyes looking up at him.

"Don't worry about me," Josiah said, wrapping an arm around Maddie's shoulders. "I'm fine. Just a little upset. I don't like people taking advantage of us."

"Papa," Maggie said. "I have an idea." When he looked down at her, she asked, "Since my new mama hasn't come, why don't you marry Ginny?"

He looked at her, and Ginny felt frozen to the spot and unable to pull her eyes away. Her heart hammered so loudly she was sure he could hear it.

"That is...that is out of the question," Josiah said, taking a deep breath. "Come, Maddie. I need to get back to work. The shop doesn't close for another two hours."

"Should we wait longer?" Maddie asked, trailing after him. "What if there's another stage?"

"There won't be," Josiah said shortly, taking her hand.

"Tomorrow?" Maddie asked, her voice getting quieter as they grew further from Ginny.

"It's doubtful. I won't wait any longer," Josiah said. "I have made up my mind. Women like that can't be trusted."

"Like what?" Maddie asked.

Ginny was now trailing behind them.

"Women who keep secrets," Josiah answered, and walked into his shop. Once Maddie was inside, he turned to Ginny. "Why don't you go home? I think I'll close my shop early today. I can still work, but I'm not in the mood to talk to customers."

Before she could answer, he'd closed the door, and the sign swayed angrily as he turned it from Open to Closed.

Ginny spun around quickly to hide her anger and her confusion. What had happened? First, they'd had what felt like the start of a moment on the stairs. Now, he was sending her away.

And what was all of that about women can't be trusted? At least, ones who kept secrets. Did that mean her? Did he think she had a secret, and that's why he'd sent her away?

It was true. She did, in a way. She had feelings for him. Feelings that were very obviously not returned or he'd have done more than look at her. He'd have said something. After all, what if he had been interested in her? He knew her! She worked for him. They'd spent hours together. Talked and laughed...He didn't know the woman who was arriving.

Ginny closed her eyes for a moment and swallowed down her hurt. This wasn't about her. This was about a man and his daughter who were hurt and confused and right now not in the best frame of mind. She needed to be kind and empathetic, not judgmental and selfish in wanting her own wishes fulfilled.

Starting the short walk home, Ginny hesitated once the tailor shop was almost out of sight. She stood, watching, almost willing Josiah to come out. To run after her or even just wave. But he didn't, and so with a heavy heart she turned and started home again.

Tomorrow might be difficult, but she was determined to pretend that nothing was bothering her. That nothing was wrong. If she tried hard enough, Ginny wondered if she could convince herself that was true. Because right now, it felt as though her very world was closing in on her.

She had been a fool wanting this job. If she'd known it would lead to heartache, she'd have just continued on her way that day and never thought twice about it. It would be far better to spend the rest of her life alone, than to spend it feeling affection for a man who didn't care for her.

Chapter 13

Josiah settled himself at a café table near the window. Ginny and Maddie had gone for a picnic. She'd offered to set something out for his lunch, but he'd declined. He'd felt the need to get away for just a short time, and had nearly flown out of his shop the moment they left.

The day had felt strange. Quite strange. When Ginny had arrived, she was all smiles and sweet. Too sweet. Too smiley. Too everything. Not having much experience with women, Josiah wondered if that meant she wasn't upset at what had happened, when he'd sent her home the day before, or if she was angry. He was almost sensing the latter, but he wasn't sure. How could one tell?

Maggie came through the kitchen door, a plate in her hand. "Here you are," she told him. "Vegetable and ham dumplings. Can I get you anything else?"

"No," Josiah answered, "thank you." As Maggie turned, an idea sprang into his mind and he asked, "Maggie, can I ask you a question?"

"You can ask anything you like," the woman replied, smiling at him. "If I answer, now, that's a different story. A woman has to have some secrets."

"Well, even if you don't, I'm not worse off than I was," Josiah told her. He frowned slightly, trying to figure out the best way to phrase his question. "When a woman is nice, overly nice, like, all smiles and too polite...what's that mean?"

Maggie looked thoughtful. "It depends. One of two things, usually. Was she also cleaning or fussing about the place? Or was she standing there fluttering her eyes at you?"

"Fussing about," Josiah said.

"Well then, I'd say she's upset and wonder just what you did. You'd better apologize," Maggie warned him. She crossed her arms. "Who was it? I'll tell you the best way how to do that. Not everybody is the same. If you do the wrong thing, it will make it much worse for you."

"N-no one," Josiah stammered.

But the café owner raised a brow. "Never took you for a man who lied," she said.

He lowered his head. He'd better just say. "Ginny," he muttered, sure his face was burning red.

"That dear girl? What did you do to make her upset?" she asked, sitting herself down across from him.

Josiah met her eyes. "That's what I'm not sure of."

"You must have done something," Maggie told him. "A woman doesn't get angry for no reason, despite what you men think. Did you say something foolish? Hurt her feelings?"

"Probably," Josiah groaned. "I have little experience with women in any capacity. In fact, it's been years since I've done more than say hello in passing or place my shopping order. I think it happened yesterday, when the woman I was waiting for at the stage didn't show. I...I might have said something out of frustration."

"Do tell," Maggie said, leaning forward, her eyes wide.

Josiah squirmed. "I don't want to be in trouble with you too," he told her. "Or have every woman in town upset at me."

Throwing her head back, Maggie chortled, "It must be real good then!"

"I was frustrated," Josiah tried to explain. He waved his arms around. "This whole situation. I can't help but feel as though I've been lied to. Taken advantage of somehow." He frowned, and then dragged his spoon through the bowl. "I uprooted Maddie and myself, my business, for this woman. And she isn't even here!"

"So, what did you say?" Maggie asked gently. "I don't plan to go spreading it around. You can trust me on that.

But you look like you need a shoulder, and I've got two of them. Well used for many a folk's problems. Let me see if I can help you."

It actually felt like she could. But Josiah couldn't meet her eyes as he whispered, "I said women like that can't be trusted. But I've a feeling she might have thought I meant all women."

"I see." Maggie leaned back, then pointed to his bowl. "Eat. It's getting cold."

Josiah wasn't feeling hungry, but he obeyed, raising the spoon to his lips. He didn't want to upset someone else. As Maggie pointed at the bowl again, he took another bite. Then another. The warm food eased some of the ache he'd been feeling. He wondered what she put in her chowder.

"Ginny's a smart girl," Maggie told him. "She's also understanding. I bet she recognizes that it's been trying for you. All of us do. I also bet she is feeling hurt and sorrowful for your sake. And," she continued, "maybe even just a little something else about you."

"That can't happen," Josiah said, quickly stuffing in another bite. He knew full well what Maggie meant. She didn't have to say it. He'd been feeling it himself since almost the moment he met Ginny.

The café door opened, and Maggie rose. She patted his shoulder before walking away. "Never say never," she told him.

Feeling almost as confused as he was before, Josiah finished his meal, then set off back to his shop. He turned the Closed sign to Open, and sat down at his workbench just as Ginny and Maddie walked in.

Both had pink cheeks and smiles, and Maddie waved at him as she ran up the stairs. Ginny started to follow, but Josiah called out, "Wait. Just a moment, please?"

She stopped and turned, one foot still on the bottom step. He hesitated, not sure why he'd asked her to stop, but he knew he had to say something. Better it be the truth, even if it was hard.

"I'm sorry if yesterday I hurt your feelings or upset you," Josiah said. "All that's been going on hasn't made me the best of people to be around nor put me in a proper mood. Yesterday, I..."

He stopped, unsure of how to finish. To his surprise, Ginny gave a small smile. A real one, even if there were hints of sadness in it.

"I understand," she told him. "You were just being you."

She walked up the stairs then, leaving Josiah wishing, for the hundredth time since he'd met her, that they could be far more than they were. If only that other woman didn't exist.

Chapter 14

After Josiah's apology, things had been better. Not perfect, but better. Ginny resigned herself to the fact that it was about as good as it was going to get. Guilt filled her too, whenever she felt like complaining, because this was trying for him. The entire situation wasn't one that she'd have enjoyed herself, were she in his shoes. Of course, Maddie was his main concern. His only concern. There was room for nothing—and no one—else.

That included her.

Should she have expected anything different? Of course not.

But why had it felt the opposite a few times? Why had he, on more than one occasion, made her feel as though he wanted to say something that could change everything between them?

"Thank you again," Josiah said, opening his shop door for her.

"I'll be back tomorrow," Ginny said, putting her lightweight shawl over her shoulders.

"Before you go," Josiah said, his voice slightly strained, "are we…well, are…"

When he didn't answer, Ginny faced him and crossed her arms. "If you are asking if we are okay," she began, "or if I'm still upset, the answers are yes and no."

"Yes and no?" he asked with a small frown. "What does that mean? You said them in order, didn't you?"

With a small laugh, Ginny squeezed his arm as she walked past and through the door. "Maybe."

"Maybe? Wait!" Josiah sputtered.

Ginny just smiled and ignored him, walking toward Maggie's Café. No, it wasn't quite right to tease him in that way, but she couldn't help it. And rather found it amusing. She didn't look over her shoulder to see his expression, though she wished she could.

A moment later, she pushed in the door of the café, causing the small bell to jingle. Carissa was bent over behind the glass case, putting pastries inside. She stood when she saw Ginny. "How are you?" she asked.

"Men are frustrating," Ginny complained to her friend.

"I know all about that," Carissa said. "I've just made a new pie recipe. Grab a table, and I'll bring us out some. You can tell me if it's worth keeping on the menu."

"I won't say no," Ginny said, and chose her favorite table, one near the books. In the winter, it was lovely to sit near the fire and read. In the summer, like now, it was nice just to be able to be surrounded by the cozy little nook Maggie had made.

Ginny didn't have to wait long. Carissa came out with a tray that held two slices of pie and two cups of tea. "That looks delicious," Ginny said, helping unload the tray. "What kind is it?"

"It's molasses and raisins," Carissa told her. "I wondered if the two would taste good together."

Taking a small bite, Ginny considered the question. The crust, as always, was flakey. "It's wonderful," she told her. "Keep it."

"I think I will," Carissa agreed. "Now, what's all this about men? And which one is frustrating you?"

"The tailor," Ginny sighed.

"Josiah?"

"That's the one." Ginny took another bite. "Sometimes I think he likes me. Other times he says things that make me think the opposite. Worse," she admitted, "I'm so selfish thinking about myself when it's obvious that he's going through a difficult time."

"Well, I don't have the most experience with men," Carissa said, "but I sure can tell you that sometimes that's how they are. It's how Duncan was. Each time I thought we were getting close, he pulled back. Sometimes even said something that hurt me."

"They must be related," Ginny muttered.

Carissa picked up her tea and looked into it. "It wasn't nice at the time. But in hindsight, I can see that he was scared."

"I'm sure Josiah is too," Ginny said. "He's been through a lot."

"You shouldn't feel bad, though, for wanting him to be clear on what he wants," Carissa told her. "Especially when it pertains to you. He really ought to just tell you. I'm sure if you think about it, it's that lack of communication that's making both you upset and him even more fearful."

"That sounds logical," Ginny sighed.

"Sometimes a man just has to figure out things for himself," Carissa told her. "But that doesn't mean you have to wait around until he decides. You have your own life too. You can't wait around forever. In fact..." Carissa smiled widely. "Duncan told me this morning one of his new ranch hands was asking about you."

"About me?" Ginny asked in surprise. That hadn't happened even once.

"Yes, he's a cute one too. A few years older than us. Maybe forget all about the one who isn't looking for love, and see if it works out with this man who wants it. We can introduce you Sunday."

It was an interesting idea. Ginny couldn't deny that a tiny sliver of excitement ran through her. She'd never caught the eye of anyone before. If this man was interested in her...

Ginny started to answer, to tell Carrissa she wasn't sure, when a carriage came down the street, slowing just past the café. That was odd. Ginny furrowed her brows. "Carissa, the stage doesn't come on Wednesdays now too, does it?"

"No," Carissa said, standing with a worried look. "We aren't prepared for such a thing."

Ginny joined her friend at the window. "I don't think it's full," she told her. "I'll help if you need me to."

The café always fed the stage passengers. Maggie and Carissa had the routine down perfectly, but the stage was usually just twice a week. An occasional third, but they were usually warned ahead of time. Because the stage stop was so short, there wasn't much time to serve the passengers, so Maggie and Carissa had the meals ready ahead of time and started to plate them as soon as the stage pulled up. As Ginny hadn't seen or heard Maggie since she'd arrived, she had the feeling the café owner wasn't there just now.

"Oh, how strange. It's just one person," Carissa said. "And she's not heading this way. Phew. That's lucky."

"Where's she going?" Ginny asked, craning her neck to see better.

Carissa shrugged and moved to the door. She opened it and stuck her head out, not seeming the least bit ashamed to stare. Ginny walked toward her and then gasped. She couldn't see the woman very well, but she was striding with great purpose right toward the tailor's shop. A simple hat covered graying hair in a bun. She wore a travel suit of brown, and in her hand was a small bag.

Every inch of Ginny tensed. Was this Josiah's wife-to-be? Had she finally arrived?

Chapter 15

When there was a knock on his shop door, Josiah looked up from the shirt he'd been wrapping in brown paper for the reverend. He didn't recognize the woman standing outside, but he crossed the shop and opened the door anyway, even if his shop was closed.

"Hello," he said. "May I help you?"

The woman looked at a paper and then at him. "Josiah Adams?" she asked, her tone one of no nonsense.

"Yes. That's me," he told her. "Is there something that I can do for you?"

"I'm actually here to help you," the woman told him. "May I come in?"

He nodded, and stepped aside. The woman walked past him and into his shop, where she glanced around. She stepped to the counter and set her bag down on top of it.

Josiah wasn't sure what to make of the woman, and tried to observe all he could, without staring at her. He didn't want to make her feel uncomfortable, but he was very curious about who she was. She was older than him by at least twenty years and looked very businesslike. Her travel suit seemed newer, as did the bag. Who was she? From another town perhaps, seeking to place an order?

"I'm sorry it took me so long to get here," the woman continued briskly. "I had delay after delay. It's most unlike me, and I feel terrible you've had to wait so long. That really doesn't bode well for my reputation."

Josiah froze. He hoped she wasn't who he suddenly suspected. His wife-to-be? She wasn't at all what he'd expected. Nor what he'd asked for. The only way to find out for sure, though, was to ask, even if the thought of her affirmative answer terrified him. "Miss," he began.

"Marston. Mrs. Marston. It is my mail-order marriage agency you applied to."

He swallowed hard. Had she been so enamored by his application that she'd kept it for herself? Did women do such things? He quickly searched the corners of his memory, trying to recall just what was so fascinating about his letter that the woman would want him for her own.

"I'm afraid there was a mistake," she told him. "And I came in person to apologize."

"A mistake?" he repeated. "What kind of mistake?"

Perhaps he should have said something like, oh, another mistake? The entire situation was a mistake. From the moment he'd filled out the application to the next when he'd arrived here, and then when the woman hadn't been here. Or arrived when she said she would. It had been one upsetting moment after another.

"The kind that made me need to come and apologize in person," the woman told him. She let out a sigh. "I'd hired a young woman to help me send out letters to men and women, letting them know where to go for their potential brides or grooms. She got very confused and ended up telling you that there was a bride here for you. That is not the case."

"There's no bride for me?" Josiah asked.

"No. The mistake happened because there was a young woman who had arrived here in Deepwater to get married some many months ago, but was rejected," Mrs. Marston said, reaching into her bag.

She pulled out a stack of papers and riffled through them. "Her name was Alyssa. Perhaps you know her? She ended up marrying a different man here. I think the confusion arose from the fact we'd promised Alyssa to find her another husband when she was ready, and the young woman in my employ misunderstood, and wanted to match her up right away. She took the letter from the stack of ineligible young women by mistake, and informed you that there was a potential bride waiting."

"Alyssa? Yes, she married the postmaster, Peter, quite some time ago, if I understand correctly," Josiah said. He shook his head. "Wait, I'm sorry. This is all a little confusing. Do you mean to tell me that there's no one here for me to marry? That I came all this way, had to reopen my business, and got my daughter's hopes up that she'd have a mother, and there isn't one for her? This entire thing was a clerical error?"

"Yes. That's just what I'm saying," the woman told him. "I'm sorry, Mr. Adams. But, please don't worry. That's part of why I came here in person. Together, we will go through the letters that I brought and send for the young woman right away. A mistake was made, but I will rectify it," Mrs. Marston said. "I will handle everything personally. In fact, I will even stay here in Deepwater until the young woman you select arrives and you are wed. It's the least I can do."

As she pulled out a stack of envelopes and began to set them before him, what she'd told him sank in.

There was no wife or mother for Maddie.

He could choose another one.

And just as suddenly, he knew that the woman he'd want to choose wouldn't be in that stack of envelopes. She wouldn't have to come from far away. Who he wanted was Ginny. If she wanted him. He wasn't sure on that part. But maybe he could try for her. See if she was willing. It would make Maddie happy to have Ginny in her life on a more permanent basis.

Truthfully, he wanted that too. But after all that had happened between them recently, he wasn't sure how to even broach the subject. Or how to help himself learn to trust in the idea of another relationship. Whenever he thought about it, he still felt pained, raw. Yet...somehow, when he thought of such a thing with Ginny, he didn't.

"Now," Mrs. Marston said, arching a brow at him, "shall I make suggestions, or would you prefer to open the letters yourself?"

Josiah hesitated, then reached for a letter. Should he look at them? Was it too late for him and Ginny? He started to remove the letter from the envelope, then he set it down. "Might I have some time to think?" he asked.

"Ahhhh. Someone here in Deepwater has caught your eye?" Mrs. Marston asked with a knowing smile.

"Perhaps," Josiah admitted. "And since I am not promised to anyone, this might be my opportunity to pursue her. I'd like to think it over, though."

"I understand," the woman told him. She scooped up the envelopes and put them back in her bag. "I'll stay the night in the café's rooms that Alyssa had stayed in while you do that. If you want to read the letters I brought with me, just find me before the stage leaves tomorrow at seven in the morning. If you need longer to think, then that is no problem. You know the agency's address and can write."

Josiah walked her to the door and watched as Mrs. Marston walked toward the café. He could see both Carissa and Ginny standing in front of it, watching the woman. He suspected they'd seen her arrive and were curious. Ginny likely thought that was the woman he was to marry, just like he'd wondered. He sucked in a deep breath. He had to do it. Had to talk to her before she assumed much more.

"Maddie," Josiah called to the backroom. "I will be right back. Don't leave the shop."

Then he left, locking the door behind him.

Chapter 16

"He's coming this way," Carissa said, nodding toward Josiah.

"So is the woman," Ginny said. She bit her lip. "She doesn't quite seem the type I'd have expected he'd have sent away for."

"She's...matronly," Carissa said. "Maybe he wanted someone not for love, but just to watch Maddie?"

"Sounds about right." Ginny nodded. Then, she put her hand to her mouth. "My goodness! Listen to us. We are practically gossiping."

"Stating facts," Maggie corrected, coming up behind them. "That's what we do around here. I agree, she doesn't seem right for him. But, Carissa, I think I smell something burning in the kitchen."

"My pie!" Carissa squealed and ran into the café.

Just then, the woman approached them. "Hello, whom do I speak with to inquire about a room for the night?"

"That would be me," Maggie said. "New to town? Come on in. I own the café and the rooms above. How long are you staying?"

Ginny wished she could have heard more, but the door closed, and the sound of her name as Josiah called out caught her attention. She hesitated, but then walked toward him. Part of her wondered if this was about Maddie, but a larger part of her knew—and her stomach sank at the thought—it was about the woman who'd just arrived.

Still, no matter what he said, she'd smile, be pleasant, and never let him know how much it pained her to do so. But also in that moment, she thought perhaps she'd ask Carissa to make her acquaintance to whoever the ranch hand was who'd asked about her. She couldn't let herself live like this, her emotions swinging one way then the next, like the pendulum on the old clock inside the general store.

"Can I speak with you a moment?" Josiah asked her, slightly breathless.

She tried to calm her apprehensiveness. "Of course."

"Can we...walk a moment?" he asked.

Ginny nodded, and they slowly walked along the street, in seemingly no direction.

"There was a woman," Josiah began without any preamble. "You might have seen her. She went into the café?"

"I did, actually," Ginny said, and hoped her voice didn't sound too strained. She was supposed to be happy for him.

"She's from the mail-order marriage company," Josiah told her.

Every muscle in Ginny clenched. She knew it. And now, he was going to tell her the wedding date. Tomorrow, likely, if the woman only wanted one night at the café. Perhaps she wanted two or three, and she'd have time to tell him and Maddie goodbye. How would she do that? How could she, without tears?

"I see," she answered, refusing to look at him, lest the pesky moisture in her eyes spring free.

"It seems there was a mistake. There was no woman waiting for me here," Josiah continued.

"Oh?" They continued to walk, then Ginny froze. "Wait." The words sank in, and that was enough to shock Ginny. She searched his face then, her voice trembling. "Does that mean you will be leaving Deepwater?"

"No, never that," Josiah said quickly, shaking his head. "Deepwater is now my home. Maddie's as well. But, there is something I need to tell you, Ginny."

"What is that?" she asked, starting to walk again slowly, not trusting herself to look at him. Her throat felt tight. Her stomach started to spin.

"I realized something. After the woman—her name is Mrs. Marston—apologized, she assured me that I could have a new bride, and she pulled out a bundle of letters for me to look through."

Ginny pressed her hands into her stomach, but it didn't ease the churning. "And, did you?" she asked softly.

"No."

She stopped walking and turned to face him. Her mouth was too dry to speak. She shivered, even though it was warm out. He hadn't looked at the letters? She didn't want to ask why, no matter how much she longed to know. What if he hadn't, because he wanted the woman who ran the agency to choose for him?

When he didn't say anything, not offering anything at all to ease her worries, and the suspense grew to more than she could bear, she finally was able to whisper, "Why?"

"Because I thought about it. There's already someone who makes me smile. Makes me sometimes forget the loneliness and pain I feel, and have felt for the last six years. There's already someone whose presence makes my house a home."

Ginny's mind spun through the possibilities. She couldn't think who he meant. Surely, after the way he'd acted, it wasn't her. She swallowed hard, closed her eyes for a moment, and steeled herself. "Is that so?" When she opened her eyes, she asked, "Who?"

He stared at her in surprise. "You, of course."

"Me?" Ginny asked. She blinked at him several times. "But I thought..."

"I know. And I'm sorry." Josiah turned away, running a hand along his jaw, and then back to her. "I have a tendency to do that, push others away and keep my pain to myself. It was never my intention to hurt you. I hope you'll believe me about that."

"I do," Ginny said. She glanced down as his hand reached for hers. His hand was larger than hers, a little rough, and wrapped around her fingers perfectly. "What now?" Ginny asked, scarcely believing he'd just said what he had.

"That I'm not sure of," he admitted. "I've not had long enough to think about that. You know how all I wanted was someone to help care for Maddie. But now, this opportunity makes me feel as though I'd like something for myself out of marriage as well. Love."

Love.

Ginny couldn't stop the broad smile on her face. She held her breath as Josiah raised her hand to his lips, and kissed her fingers.

"Will you give me just a little time, Ginny? Knowing that my heart is only for you? I promise it is, but let me have a little bit to figure out how to be the man you want and need, and how to let myself learn to trust and love again? You deserve the best of me."

"Of course I will," Ginny said in a whisper, watching as he gave her a shy smile, then hurried away again toward his shop.

She wasn't sure what to think. In a daze, she walked back toward her house. No one would be there, and she was glad of that. Her parents and younger siblings had left for a few days to visit her oldest brother, so she could just sit and think.

Relive each of the words Josiah had told her.

Smile and squeal and giggle without anyone staring at her.

Wonder if it had been a dream.

But, if it was, Ginny didn't want to wake up.

Chapter 17

Josiah stuck his head out of his shop door, worriedly looking around. It had started to rain, and Ginny and Maddie should have been home by now.

Maddie had pleaded with him to let her go to the forest and pick the wild berries that grew there. She and Ginny had done it once before, but they'd been back well before it was his shop's closing time. It was about time to put away his scissors and needle for the day, and they were nowhere around. That, and the fact the skies were menacing looking, had him feeling more than concerned.

Hurriedly, he closed his shop and walked outside in the direction of the woods. The wind had picked up, and leaves flew along the street. Yes, there was a storm coming all right. They would be on their way back to avoid it. Surely, he'd meet up with them.

But he didn't.

Josiah ventured carefully into the forest, uncertain where the berry patch was. He called out several times, but there was no reply. The forest was larger than he'd imagined, and as Josiah stood there in the rain that first plopped gently, but then beat down with a vengeance, he felt scared. He also would have no idea how to find his way back, if he lost sight of the town that was barely visible through the trees.

He searched, continuing to call. The rain lightened, but fog lingered, heavily in some spots, trapped within the trees. Were Ginny and Maddie lost in it? He called out again. "Ginny! Maddie! Where are you?" But as before, there was no answer.

Where was Maddie? Where was Ginny? He called out to them again and waited for an answer. There was none. He was sure something had happened.

He turned back toward the town, pushing his wet hair from his forehead. It would be dark in a few hours. Maybe he could get some help from a few of the other men. If they had gotten lost or someone had gotten hurt, they would need help. He might be unfamiliar with the woods, but he was sure others would know it like the backs of their hands.

Josiah tried to ignore the little voice whispering how he couldn't trust anyone with Maddie. How he shouldn't have trusted Ginny or let Maddie out of his sight. "You are wrong!" he told himself in a growl. "Ginny can be trusted. She didn't take Maddie away. She wouldn't, not after I told her how I feel about her! They are...they are just lost and I must find them."

But did she feel the same? In his absolute terror that the words had been pulled from him, Josiah realized he'd left without hearing her answer.

The church was close by. Josiah hoped the reverend was there. He could suggest who would know the forest best. Josiah glanced upward. The rain had picked up again, and the dark clouds made the hour seem much later than it was. Depending on how deep in the woods Ginny and Maddie were, it would be even darker.

A crash of thunder sounded, and Josiah ran as quickly as he could on the muddy patches forming on the path. Cold rain pelted him, making him shiver as it ran down his collar. Ginny and Maddie would be cold too. It was unlikely they had shelter. And if they were wet, they might get sick. Deepwater had no doctor yet, though the reverend had been trying to find one.

The church now in front of him, Josiah burst in, sending a silent apology to God for dripping on the church floors.

"Reverend? Gabriel! Are you here?" Josiah wasn't surprised his voice held panic.

"I'm here," Gabriel's voice came, and a moment later, he and Laura had rushed out of the small back room where Gabriel's office was. "Josiah, what's wrong?"

"Ginny took Maddie to pick berries in the woods," Josiah said, his words in a rush. "They should have been back hours ago. And now…"

"I'll get lanterns and blankets," Laura said, hurrying away.

"Don't worry," Gabriel said. He went to the front of the church and rang the bell that hung there.

The sound was loud, urgent, and it struck Josiah that other than on Sunday mornings, he'd never heard it before. Would others know what it meant?

"Help will come," Gabriel said, pausing to speak over the sound, then he rang it again.

At the front of the church, Laura appeared with several lanterns and an armful of blankets. "I'll go to the café," she told Josiah and Gabriel. She looked at Josiah and explained, "That's where the women will gather to do our part, and wait for you men to get there and update us."

"I don't know the area. Is there any shelter for them?" Josiah asked, watching as Laura ran from the church into the downpour. He could see people dashing toward the church, men, some with lanterns, others with alarm on their faces.

Gabriel nodded. "There are some homes. Perhaps they found shelter there. We'll arrange for everyone to split up, and both go to those houses on the outskirts as well as search the area. Would they have gone anywhere else?"

"I doubt it," Josiah said. "They were going after some of those wild berries. Ginny has always been truthful and conscientious of where I will let Maddie go."

"Then that is where you and Hank and I will start," Gabriel told him.

The church had filled by then with men. Gabriel stood in the front, and said, "Josiah's daughter and Ginny went to the woods and should have returned well before now. You all know what they look like. We need to split up. Hank?"

The man who, Josiah had recently learned, was a former lawman who still acted in that capacity for the town, nodded, and started pointing to various men. "Dirk, you, Duncan, Brett, and Joe, visit the houses on the outskirts. Peter, Cal, Kevin, and Jim, go to the ones nearest the forest. Gabriel, Josiah, and I will head to the berry patch. The rest of you search the woods. You know the drill, three whistles if you find something, one whistle if you are heading back to the café. Crow call if you need help."

Gabriel led them in a quick prayer for safety and the recovery of Ginny and Maddie. Josiah's eyes pricked with tears as fear swarmed around in his gut. He knew this wasn't his fault or Ginny's, not that he knew of, but he was still scared. The voice kept whispering to him that he knew better than to trust someone. What if they couldn't find them? And if they did, what if they were hurt?

Josiah knew if anything happened to his daughter, he would never be the same. It had been foolish of him to open his heart and allow someone to lower his defenses. This is what it got him. More pain.

The men dispersed quickly, lanterns and oilskins and blankets in their arms.

"I don't know how to thank you," Josiah said as he watched them. "All of you."

"It's what we do for our own," Hank assured him, thumping his shoulder. "Now, let's go get those girls of yours."

Josiah nodded. Yes, they were his. At least, he'd wanted Ginny to be. Was he too late?

Fear for her safety and Maddie's filled him. The three walked abreast, so as to miss less in the pouring rain. The other men had a serious look on their faces, and Josiah was sure his matched. A thought echoed in his mind, banging like the toy drum Maddie had begged for years before and played with constantly.

He'd only just made things right with Ginny, and hoped to have a future with her. Had he lost her now? And what kind of father was he, failing to protect his own child?

Lightning streaked across the sky and thunder shook the ground with a low rumble. Long shadows from the lantern made everything look sinister. It reminded Josiah that there were dangers in these woods. He should have never let them go in them alone.

Chapter 18

"Ginny, I'm cold," Maddie whimpered, hugging her small arms around her. "I wish I'd brought my shawl you made me."

"I'm cold too," Ginny said, wishing very much for hers as well. "But aren't we lucky that we've found a place to wait out this rain?"

Maddie's nose crinkled as she sat tucked into the tree's hollow. Ginny tried to keep the look of calm on her face, but in truth she was scared. It was starting to get dark, and the rain had not stopped. She was faced with a terrible choice. Try to find their way back in the dark and risk getting hurt or even more lost, or wait until morning.

Either way, she knew Josiah must be near panic by now. Maddie was his whole world. She knew he hardly let her out of his sight. And now this. He'd never forgive her.

What kind of person was she? Getting herself and Maddie lost. There was no way Josiah would ever want to consider a future with her now.

Ginny wrapped an arm around Maddie, trying to provide a little warmth. She closed her eyes for a moment, trying to piece together what had happened.

They'd been there, picking berries. Then, a bear had lumbered toward them. She and Maddie had slowly backed away, trying to get out of sight of it. That's when the forest had filled with the strangest fog. It made it difficult to see, and soon they were in a part of the woods Ginny had never been in before.

The fog had lifted slightly, then it started to rain. Then pour. They were turned around, and without shelter. It was fortunate this large tree had been nearby, with several large branches that blocked most of the rain.

She had shivered while doing it, but Ginny had gathered a few fallen branches with leaves, and set them in a sort of makeshift shelter around the tree. It wasn't much, but it had helped to block even more of the rain.

Now, she just needed to figure out what to do. Maddie's short legs and fast-tiring feet wouldn't let them go much further, even if they did try. They were also both exhausted, and it was well past the evening meal time.

"I wish we still had the berries," Maddie said. "I'm hungry."

"So was that bear," Ginny said. "I wonder if he ate them all."

"I'd rather he eat the berries than me," Maddie said seriously.

"I would much rather that too," Ginny said. "Usually, we don't get animals that close to town." She looked down at Maddie. "Don't worry. I bet your papa is looking for us right now."

Maddie nodded, but Ginny wasn't sure she believed her. She hoped Josiah would be looking for them. He was their only hope, since her parents wouldn't be home to notice she wasn't. No one would have known she was missing, had she not been with Maddie, who was expected to return.

Time moved slowly. At least, that's what it felt like. The rain began to taper off, but the night was cloudy, and there was only a hint of the moon Ginny knew was there, illuminating the edges of a cloud.

"Try to sleep. Morning will come quicker, and then we can make our way home," Ginny said.

"I can't sleep," Maddie cried. "I'm scared and cold and hungry."

So am I, Ginny thought. She wanted nothing more than to be before a roaring fire, wrapped in a blanket, and with something warm in her stomach.

To distract Maddie, she told her stories, quietly, so as not to attract more animals from their voices, and when at last the girl fell asleep, many, many stories later, Ginny wished—not for the first time—that they'd never even entered the forest. She wasn't very familiar with it, and it was far larger than she'd imagined.

Ginny closed her eyes, and warm tears trickled from under her lashes. Her body ached with weariness. But how could she sleep in this kind of situation? She was responsible for caring for Maddie, but she'd failed her. Failed Josiah.

In the distance, Ginny thought she heard a whistle, and stared into the darkness toward where she thought the sound was coming from. Was that a light? She wasn't sure. Ginny leaned forward, squinting into the darkness. Was someone looking for them? Hope rose, but then quickly fled. She didn't dare leave Maddie to find out, and the tiny spark was gone now. It must have been her imagination.

She sighed, and leaned back into their shelter again. Tomorrow, when the sun rose, that would at least give her a general direction to go. She knew the position of the sun each morning both in correlation to her parents' home and Josiah's shop. That should be enough to get them started along the right way back to town.

Unless she went the absolute opposite way. But sooner or later, they'd reach a house or a town or someone to help them.

She hoped.

While most everyone out here was kind, there were a few living on the outskirts of Deepwater who didn't welcome strangers or trespassers. Right now, she and Maddie were likely both.

Nearby, an animal howled. Ginny shuddered.

Yes. The sun would get them back home. Then she'd never go back into this forest again. That is, if they survived the night.

The animal howled again. Next to her, Maddie stirred, and then she screamed.

Chapter 19

"We should stop for the night," Hank said.

"We can't!" Josiah nearly shouted. "I'll keep going on my own."

Gabriel laid a hand on his arm. "He didn't say we were. He said we should. However, it appears none of us have the sense we should. I would like to take just a moment to meet with the others, if we are going to continue the search. Splitting up didn't seem to do the trick."

Josiah nodded. He agreed. The area was so large, it would be easy to miss them, especially if Ginny and Maddie were lying hurt or had stopped to rest and fell asleep.

The urgency to find them filled him. The earlier voice had fled, leaving only a singular thought in his head. He didn't want to be without either of them. He loved them both too much.

"I found something!" Hank called, and held up a bucket. "This yours?"

Josiah looked at the wooden bucket with hesitation. Was it? "I can't say for certain," he finally said. "I've never paid much attention to my bucket, but there are berries at the bottom."

"That's what I was thinking," Hank said, rubbing at his jaw. "There's signs of a bear here too, and recent."

Josiah's stomach churned, and every inch of his being felt sick. "A bear?"

"Don't worry," Gabriel quickly assured him. "If they came across it, it was likely as scared of them as they were of it. I bet that's how they got lost, trying to slip away."

"They're still alive, I'm sure," Hank said. "Or else we'd be seeing signs of an attack here, and I don't."

Josiah nodded, but didn't feel much better. All he could think about right now was Ginny and Maddie, alone and cold and scared, a bear chasing after them.

Hank let out a whistle, loud enough to leave Josiah's ears ringing. Echoes of whistles sounded throughout the forest. A few moments later, all of the men who'd been searching were gathered.

"We're going to keep looking," Hank said. "But we've got to get a new plan to find them. They are no doubt here somewhere, and we are overlooking them."

"If only we had a little more light," Dirk said. "These lanterns aren't throwing the kind of brightness we need."

"I understand if you need rest," Josiah said, stepping closer. "I can't ask you to keep looking. Please, take some time to eat if you need to."

"We'll do that when the job is done," Duncan assured him. "None of us are going anywhere."

Josiah swallowed down the lump in his throat, and nodded his thanks. It wasn't enough, but it was all he could offer right now.

An animal's howl in the distance was enough to make the hairs on his neck stand up straight. It howled again, and then it was followed by something human. A scream. Though faint, Josiah knew it.

"Maddie!" Josiah shouted, running toward the sound. "That's Maddie!"

The crashing of boots on leaves and branches filled Josiah's ears as they all raced in the direction of the scream. "Maddie!" he shouted. "Ginny!"

All around him, the other men did the same, their weariness fading at the hope they might have found them.

"Wait!" Gabriel yelled. "We'll never hear them with all of our shouting and running. Josiah, just you. Call to them."

"Maddie! Ginny!" Josiah shouted, projecting his voice as much as he could.

"Here!" a faint cry came back. "We're here!"

It was Ginny!

The men moved forward again, navigating or tripping over fallen branches and holes in the ground from animals. Every few yards Josiah called out again, and they reoriented themselves based on where they heard Ginny reply. Relief filled Josiah as her voice grew louder. They were almost there. He'd found them!

As they drew closer, the lanterns casting more light as the men circled the area, Josiah could see two slight figures standing there, one of them much smaller than the other and huddled into the first.

"Josiah?"

Ginny's voice, so hesitant, so fearful, sent a surge of happiness through him. He rushed toward her. "Yes! Are you hurt?"

"We're fine," Ginny assured him. "Just cold and hungry."

"We've got blankets," Gabriel said, stepping forward and offering them.

Josiah wrapped one around Maddie then hugged her tightly, while Ginny wound one around her shoulders. Both Ginny and his daughter were wet from the rain and shivering.

"I'm glad you are safe," Josiah said, releasing Maddie only long enough to take Maddie's hand in one of his, and Ginny's in his other. "I was so worried."

"We didn't mean to get lost," Ginny said tearfully. "There was a bear and we got turned around."

"You're safe, and that's all that matters," Josiah said.

"I'll fetch a wagon and take you back home," Gabriel said. "Laura will come with us. She's at the café waiting with something to warm you up."

"Thank you," Ginny said tiredly.

Josiah swung Maddie into his arms for the trip back. They trudged through the dark woods, lit only by the meager lanterns. There was so much Josiah wanted to say, but with this many others around, he didn't feel he could. After about twenty minutes of walking, the edge of Deepwater appeared, and soon after the café.

Everyone hurried inside, and Maggie snatched up Maddie, making a fuss over her and giving her a plate with thick slices of bread with jam. Ginny sat tiredly with a cup of tea and her own bread and jam.

Gabriel had gone to get the wagon, so Josiah knew he wouldn't have long before she was taken back home. He sat at the table with his daughter and Ginny, grateful to have them both safe.

"I'm sorry to have worried you," Ginny said, her voice low. "I'm sure you were thinking the worst."

Josiah thought for a moment before he answered. "At first, I was," he agreed. "But I didn't like that voice. What went through my mind the most, though, was how I didn't want to be without either of you. I love you. Both of you."

Ginny's cheeks pinked, but the smile that lit her face warmed every inch of him. He was about to say more, to ask her a very important question, when Laura said, "Are you ready? We'll take you back and see you settled in."

"Yes, thank you," Ginny said. She took the last sip of her tea and smiled at Josiah apologetically.

But as she left, she bent down as she walked past. "I love you too."

Chapter 20

A loud knocking on the door startled Ginny. She hurried toward it, wondering who would be here at this hour. She was dressed, luckily, because she was planning to spend the day with Maddie, like always.

Her body still ached from her time sitting against the tree, and she was tired, only having had a few hours of sleep, but Maddie was her responsibility, so she'd be there, even if tiredness nearly consumed her.

Fighting back a yawn, Ginny opened the front door, and was surprised to see Josiah standing in front of her. Instantly, her fatigue fled. "Is everything okay?" she asked. "Where's Maddie?"

"With Maggie," Josiah said. "Or, rather, Maggie is at the shop with Maddie. I asked her to watch her for a moment. Maddie's still sleeping."

Ginny nodded. She'd imagine so. It had been only a few hours before dawn when they were rescued.

"Is she doing all right, after last night?" she asked worriedly.

"She is. But that's what I wanted to talk to you about," Josiah said.

Ginny nodded, and lowered her eyes, sure he was going to tell her how she shouldn't have taken Maddie there. Likely, he'd even changed his mind about wanting her to give him time to consider a relationship. She'd nearly lost the most important thing to him, his daughter. Of course he'd be upset, once he had time to think about it.

To her surprise, he took her hands in his. "I have to tell you something," Josiah said. "I didn't sleep at all. Instead, I just thought over and over how I couldn't wait for daylight so I could speak with you."

"What is it?" Ginny asked.

"Marry me. Today."

Ginny's jaw dropped. "To-today?"

"Yes. Or," he frowned, "I forgot. You'll want your parents back. Next week? Will you marry me next week? I don't want to spend another moment without you. You complete us, Ginny. I want you for Maddie's mother; she does too. But most importantly of all, I want you for my wife. You are the one that I love."

"You...you are not angry with me?" Ginny asked. "I thought...after all..."

"I could never be," Josiah said. "Maddie told me how you cared for her. How you protected her, kept her warm, helped her not be scared. I have seen that the love I have for my daughter is matched by yours. I know you would have done anything to keep her safe. What happened wasn't your fault. But it made me realize that I have wasted too much time."

Ginny searched his face. "I don't want you to feel rushed or forced. You'd asked for time. If—"

He shook his head. "You are nothing like Celina was. I've known that all along. I also know that I can't live in the past. By doing so, I've missed out on too much. Who knows how much time any of us have? I don't want to waste another moment. I love you, Ginny. There is no one else for me. I realize that. Please, say yes?"

Ginny's smile was so wide, her face hurt. "Oh! Yes, Josiah! Next week."

He pulled her into his arms and kissed her gently. "I can't wait," he said. "I'm sure you've things you want to plan. Do you want the day off?"

"Not at all," Ginny said. "I'll take Maddie along with me. First, I'm going to ask Maggie and Carissa to make the cake. Then, I'll go speak with the reverend."

"That sounds wonderful," Josiah said. "If you are ready now, we can walk back together?"

"Yes, just let me get my shawl," Ginny said.

She hurried to grab it, then closed and locked the door behind her. She and Josiah walked back to town, hand in hand. Happiness filled every inch of Ginny, from the top of her head down to her toes.

"I never imagined this would happen, the day I met you," she told him.

"I didn't either," he said, squeezing her hand. "But I realize I'm the luckiest man in Deepwater. You've said yes."

Ginny laughed, her heart feeling light. The shop came into view, and Maggie opened the door with a wide smile.

"Do I sense a wedding?" the café owner asked eagerly.

"You do," Ginny said. "And I hope you'll make the cake?"

"Come over as soon as you can," Maggie said, clapping her hands together. "Carissa and I will get all of your ideas." She glanced at Josiah. "Maddie just woke up, and she's eating some flapjacks I whipped up."

"Thank you," Josiah said. "I appreciate you coming on such short notice. And for making her breakfast."

Maggie waved her hand dismissively. "That's what we do for our own here," she told him. Then she smiled at the two of them, and nodded. "Looks like Deepwater brought another couple together."

"Looks like it," Ginny said with a laugh.

"I'll see you soon," Maggie said, and left for her café.

Josiah held the door, and Ginny walked inside. "I'm happy I said yes to that letter," Josiah told her. "And I'm even happier it was a mix-up, and I got to have you."

"So am I," Ginny told him, walking up the narrow wooden stairs. She pushed open the door and saw Maddie's sleepy face. "Hello, Maddie. Are you up for a day out?"

"What are we going to do?" Maddie asked eagerly.

Ginny glanced at Josiah, and then grinned at Maddie. "Your papa has asked me to marry him, and we are going to do it next week. Maggie is going to make our cake. I thought you might want to help pick it out today."

Maddie jumped up and hugged her, then burst into tears.

"What's wrong?" Josiah asked, concern in his voice.

"I'm happy," Maddie said. "I've waited so long for you, Mama."

Tears sprang to Ginny's eyes as well, and she kneeled to wrap her arms around Maddie's small frame. Josiah did the same and together, the soon-to-be family clung to each other.

"I'll never leave you," Ginny promised. "Either of you. I love you both, forever."

Epilogue

Three years later

Josiah stretched for a moment, then bent over his needle and thread again. He'd never been so busy in his life. Word of his skill in making clothes for men had gotten around, and many from towns as far away as two hours stopped by. He'd had to hire an extra pair of hands, and that was in addition to Ginny helping him in the evenings by cutting out the fabric and pinning it.

Ginny.

Every moment with her had been better than the last. The moment they'd said "I do," everything had felt complete. He'd never felt so happy, and could tell Maddie, who was now nearing ten, felt the same. They'd had a little boy last year, and Maddie adored him, and was just as much his mother as Ginny was.

"You look lost in thought."

Josiah startled, then smiled at Ginny. She held a tray, and he eagerly moved his material. "Thank you! I'm hungry, and whatever that is smells wonderful."

She set down the food, a bowl of some sort of stew, cornbread, and some cookies, then sat next to him. "Dirk is going to love this shirt," she said, nodding at the rich red fabric.

"I understand Samantha is getting something similar made in a dress, and they'll perform at the next Christmas program," he said.

"I can't wait," Ginny said. There was a crash from upstairs, and she stood quickly, hurrying away.

Josiah smiled as he watched her go, then turned his attention to the window, where a couple strolled past hand in hand and laughing. He no longer felt sad or that painful tightness in his chest when that happened. Instead, he felt proud that he had the same. Someone to share his days with.

Deepwater sure had a way of bringing people together. Everyone who'd told him that had been right. He might not have believed it at first, but now he did.

"I wonder who will find love here next," he said, as he watched a few men and women he knew were single walk the street.

Whoever it was, he hoped they'd be as lucky in love as he was. With someone who filled his life with happiness, and chased away the darkness of his past. If they let them, because that was the real trick, wasn't it? Opening your heart to new people and experiences, even if they were frightening at times.

Laughter from upstairs caught his attention, and Josiah stood, heading that way to embrace his family once more before he continued work. He still had lost time to make up for, and he no longer wasted a moment of it.

Note from Author

Thank you for taking the time to read *Mail-Order Tailor*.
Could I ask for one small favor? Reviews like yours on
Amazon mean so much to me and help others to find my
books! Even just a single line means a lot!

Also...

Want a FREE book?

Stop by my website to get your no strings attached **FREE
book**. It's my gift to you, as a thank you for reading this
one.

www.sarahlambbooks.com

***

Are you curious about the woman Josiah was sent to marry, Alyssa? Read Alyssa and Peter's story in *Alyssa's Desperate Plan*.

"Yer too small on the top. I want a bigger woman."

Alyssa Moore never expected *that* to be the reason her prospective groom turned her away after one look. Now, with almost no money and no family to turn to for help, she's stuck waiting in a small town until the mail-order bride agency that sent her finds another match. She's embarrassed to seek help because that isn't her only mortifying situation, but it's all she can do.

When an upset woman finds him to ask for help posting a letter, Peter West is more than curious about her. As he learns more, he wonders...what would happen if her letter didn't post? At least for a few days. Would she consider staying there, with someone like him? He knows it's pointless. A beautiful woman like that wouldn't want a man like him.

As Alyssa becomes desperate and Peter tries to summon his courage, they'll each discover there's far more to a person than meets the eye—and that friendship and love can blossom in the most unexpected of ways.

Find it here:

https://www.amazon.com/Alyssas-Desperate-Rejected -Mail-Order-Brides-ebook/dp/B0CN8FKZX7

And then check out some of the other stories set in Deepwater.

Trapped in Deepwater (Laura and Reverand Gabriel Sullivan's story)

Find it here:

https://www.amazon.com/Trapped-Deepwater-Christmas-Bride-Dilemma-ebook/dp/B0C74R6NW6

Away in Deepwater (Samantha and Dirk's story)

Find it here:

https://www.amazon.com/Away-Deepwater-Christmas-Sweethearts-Historical-ebook/dp/B0DM6SPJDJ

Cherry Cheese Pie by Carissa (Carissa and Duncan's story)

Find it here:

https://www.amazon.com/Cherry-Cheese-Pie-Carissa-Holiday-ebook/dp/B0DDQJYMPT

Want more Mail-Order Husbands? You might enjoy *Mail-Order Teacher* and *Mail-Order Gambler*

Mail-Order Teacher

Find it here:

https://www.amazon.com/Mail-Order-Teacher-Honorable-Sarah-Lamb-ebook/dp/B0CQ3WZCFN

Mail-Order Gambler

Find it here:

https://www.amazon.com/Mail-Order-Gambler-Husbands-Sarah-Lamb-ebook/dp/B0D7FWMLDP

About the Author

Sarah writes captivating characters and clean romance that's anything BUT boring! From heartbreaking moments to heartwarming tales, get swept away in either historical or small town romance that pulls you in until the last page.

Nestled in the Blue Ridge Mountains of Virginia where she's married to her Texan husband, you'll find Sarah creating her next book, homeschooling her two boys, or volunteering in her community.

There are other great books in this series as well!

Find all the Mail-Order Husband books on Amazon!

Want more of Sarah's books? Find them all on Amazon!

https://www.amazon.com/stores/Sarah-Lamb/author/B098H3SGLK